SCI-SHORTS II

by Mark Roman

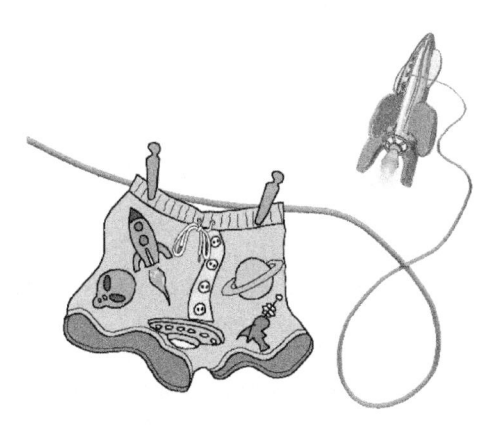

A collection of humorous science fiction stories
with illustrations by Corben Duke

Grinning Bandit Books
http://grinningbandit.webnode.com

First published in 2023 by
Grinning Bandit Books
Copyright © Mark Roman 2023

The stories collected here are purely fictional, as are the characters (including aliens). Any names that relate to any persons (or aliens) are purely coincidental.

All rights reserved.
No part of this book may be reproduced or transmitted in any form or by any means, electronic, digital or mechanical, without permission in writing from the copyright owner.

ISBN: 9798866287376

Cover design by Corben Duke and Mark Roman

For Gareth

Also by Mark Roman (with Corben Duke)

The Worst Man on Mars

Sci-Fi Shorts

Contents

Tunnel Vision	1
Magi-water	14
Well Read	34
Space Tourists	42
Intuition	58
Rock 100	66
Libel	87
Quick Sale	101
Righter of Wrongs	109
Spy Human	127
Acknowledgements	145
About the Author	146
Extract from Sci-Fi Shorts	147
The Man Who Saved the World (Kind Of)	149

Tunnel Vision

The moment I spotted him I knew I was in trouble, big trouble.

Heading down the train aisle in his dark blue uniform, swinging his electronic ticket-reading machine like a cowboy gunslinger, was Inspector Zero Tolerance. The burly, stony faced one with the sarcastic put-downs and not a shred of human empathy. Towering over the passengers, with a fresh crew cut, and a scar down his right cheek, he eyed the commuters to his left and right with his habitual disdain as he dismissed their proffered (and valid) tickets in evident disappointment.

My heart stopped as I realized he would not be disappointed with me. Only seconds earlier, it had hit me that my annual season ticket had expired the day before. I should have renewed it at the station, but had forgotten, and now I would suffer the consequences.

Just what I needed after a truly miserable week at work.

"Tickets, please," he boomed as he came to a halt next

to me, a barely suppressed smirk playing about his lips. He knew, of course he knew. He'd seen my annual pass countless times and no doubt had the expiry date seared into his memory. These days he rarely bothered to ask; he'd just nod or wink as he passed. No doubt biding his time, waiting for the day he'd be able to pounce.

And pounce he just had.

With trembling fingers, I handed over my now-invalid permit to travel and flashed a wan smile at him. I watched hopefully as he examined it, praying for the impossible chance that he had somehow forgotten the date.

But it was like he was admiring a particularly sought-after collectors' item.

"Expired," he said at last with a sigh, probably intended as sympathetic, but coming across like a triumphant fist-pump.

"I hadn't realized ..." I stammered.

He lowered himself into the seat opposite and took out his pad of penalty notices and his pen. He threw me an insincere this-is-going-to-hurt-me-more-than-it-is-you look. Somewhat symbolically, the carriage darkened as the train plunged into a tunnel.

"I'd lost track of the date," I continued. "I'll renew it as soon as we get to Cambridge. Honest."

He nodded as he jotted a few details on his pad. "'Course you will, sir. 'Course you will. I expect you'll be making a beeline for the ticket office before the train's even stopped. Name?"

My heart sank. No point arguing.

Many a time I'd seen him collar a forgetful or confused passenger plus, of course, the occasional out-and-out fare-dodger. Each time he'd listen to their genuine, or made up, stories with the same air of scepticism, nodding occasionally and seemingly sympathetically. But, however heart-breaking their story, however reasonable their excuse, however believable, he'd always make some sort of quip before calmly and coldly slapping a hefty fine on them. Irrespective of age, gender, nationality, proficiency in English, or medical condition. The man was a heartless fiend.

And now he had his sights set on me. "Stephen Bradshaw," I sighed, the name catching in my throat.

As he wrote it down in the appropriate box, the train emerged from the tunnel and suddenly the brakes slammed on with a deafening shriek as the wheels skidded on the rails. I was thrown back against my seat and pinned there. Then, as though in slow motion, I watched in horror as the ticket inspector's huge bulk flew towards me, crushing me and driving all the air from my lungs.

For a long five seconds I could not breathe as the train's brakes continued to screech and two hundred pounds of humourless job's-worth pressed into my chest. Then the carriage started jumping and swaying, as though no longer running on rails, and Zero Tolerance and I found ourselves rubbing up against one another in what, under different circumstances, would have been construed as a most unseemly manner.

Finally, the train ground to a halt, and we were able to disengage.

"Sorry," we both mumbled, flustered by our recent intimacy. Hastily, he returned to the seat opposite. I handed back his electronic machine which had somehow found its way into my armpit.

But things were about to become rather surreal. As I composed myself, I saw Zero's jaw drop in horror and his eyes bulge as he stared out of the window.

"Cripes!" he exclaimed in a breaking voice. "Not again!"

I followed his gaze, and initially couldn't grasp what I was looking at because the scene before me was so totally bewildering. Gone was the doomy grey sky and dreary Essex countryside of endless fields and hedges that we had been travelling through, and in its place was a delightful, bucolic scene, bursting with dazzling greens, brightly coloured flowers, and a brilliant blue and cloudless sky. The sunlight filtering through the lush foliage of the trees dappled the velvety grass with its brightness. Many of the trees had unfeasibly large fruit hanging from them, positively radiating their ripeness, and demanding to be picked and gorged on.

But what really caught the eye were the people. Young people, beautiful people, fresh and lively. Men and women, either naked or clad in skimpy undergarments, whose skin and hair spanned the colours of the rainbow. Some were dancing, others relaxed in the sunshine, some swam in the deep blue lagoon, while many engaged in the sorts of activities naked men and women tend to engage in. Each seemed to have a hazy glow around them, and most were spectacularly well endowed in the appropriate regions, which bobbled enticingly as they moved in their languid, carefree way.

"What the …?" I managed to say.

Here and there stood trestle tables laden with the most delicious looking foods and drinks, while scattered on the ground were variously sized balls and bats and rackets, and other equipment designed for outdoor fun and games, as well as some for indoor fun and games. A heady fragrance filled my nostrils from the sliding window above my head; a mixture of flower smells and culinary aromas.

The inspector was shaking his head in disapproval as he continued to mutter, "Not again, not again."

Then he turned to me and, on seeing my perplexed expression, explained, "We've entered another dimension. Or an alternative reality. Or parallel universe. Or something."

"We've what?" I asked, desiring a more plausible-sounding explanation than that.

He sighed. "Same thing happened a couple of months back. A scientist passenger tried to explain it to me. Something about passing through a rift in the membrane separating two universes. We lost Gordon the driver ..." He stiffened as he said this, eyes widening. Then he jumped to his feet and, without another word, sped down the aisle towards the driver's cabin, pounding on the door. "Phil!" he called. "You alright in there, Phil?"

Something caught my eye outside. A beautiful blonde, with pale purple skin, was smiling and waving to me from outside. Clad in lacy lingerie, she was utterly stunning. She advanced through the lush grass towards the train, taking slow, languorous strides.

I swallowed hard, unable to breathe, nor take my eyes off her. As I drank in her loveliness, she signalled me to come join her. Drawn by her strong allure I leaned forwards, only to thump my nose on the glass. I pulled back, rubbing it, embarrassed, but my sense of foolishness abated at the sight of her giggling.

I was dimly aware that many of the other beautiful people outside were also smiling and beckoning to the other passengers on the train. But I only had eyes for her.

I had to meet her!

I sprang from my seat and headed for the driver's cabin just as the ticket inspector disappeared inside. I sped up, but after only a few steps I was waylaid by a distraught Japanese couple surrounded by bulky suitcases.

"Why we stop?" demanded the man.

I tried to pass but he grabbed my arm and repeated his question.

"Leaves on the line," I replied with a tight smile.

Clearly the joke was lost on him, and his distress only increased. "We miss our plane!"

"Seriously?" I said, indicating the world outside. "That's what you're worried about?"

Normally I would have been sympathetic, explaining they were on the wrong train heading in the wrong direction – a common enough mistake I had seen dozens of tourists make in the past. This was the Cambridge train, and they should have changed at Bishops Stortford for the Stansted Express.

But the man just stared at me. His wife, who had glanced outside and almost choked on what she saw, was tugging at his sleeve to get him to look for himself. But he ignored her, seemingly keener to argue with me.

I took a deep breath. "Look, I'm just going to ask the driver. OK?"

His wife uttered some hurried words in Japanese, which gave me the chance to escape. I felt I had wasted enough time already. I needed to get to my blonde beauty before she went away.

I reached the driver's cabin and slipped inside, totally unprepared for what I encountered there. The ticket inspector and the driver were engaged in a no-holds-barred wrestling match, the latter pinned against the dashboard. Both grunted and groaned as they grappled with one another. A fist would occasionally pound into a midriff, or a leg attempt to trip another leg. The entangled pair lumbered first one way until they hit a wall, and then another until they encountered another obstruction.

"What's going on?" I cried, but they were too engrossed in their private brawl to respond.

"No, Phil, no," the inspector kept imploring.

"I have to go out there, Ron," the driver wailed back. "Let me go, Ron. I want to go."

I quickly grasped the situation. The driver, a large man, bald, and no longer in the first flush of youth, was reaching out with stubby fingers towards a young, smiling beauty outside, while being held back by the burly ticket inspector.

Suddenly, the driver stopped his struggles and cried, "Look, there's Gordon!" He pointed out of the side window. Ron the ticket inspector released his hold and looked. A middle-aged man with greying hair and a significant paunch stood waving at us, totally naked but for the voluptuous brunette draped around him.

"Good grief, you're right. It's Gordon!" exclaimed Ron.

"Gordon?" I asked.

"I told you," said the ticket inspector. "Gordon. The driver we lost last time we were here."

Phil turned to him with wild eyes. "See? Gordon's

fine. He's been here for several weeks and he's smiling and waving and happy. His life is good, and he's beckoning us over. I'm going!"

With a burst of energy, he twisted himself free of Ron's grasp and in a flash opened the door and jumped down before Ron could react.

"No, Phil!" cried the inspector, grasping at his retreating figure. "We can't lose any more drivers! Come back."

But Phil was being led away by two beautiful females and one beautiful male. The females were hugging and kissing him, while the male was helping him out of his clothing. I'd never been so jealous of another man in all my life.

I noticed that my own blonde beauty was standing below the open door, smiling, beckoning to me, and forming a heart with her fingers. I had to go to her.

But the inspector was too quick, blocking my way before I'd had a chance to move.

"Oh no you don't," he said, closing the door.

"But I must go to her!" I begged. I blew her a kiss and she blew one back, which increased my urge to join her.

"No, Stephen," said Ron, tightening his grip on me.

I was momentarily taken aback at his having remembered my name, but then I started pleading my case.

Of course, as I've said, the man was heartless and totally impervious to emotional entreaties of any kind. But I had to try.

"Please let me go. I have a boring dead-end job with no career prospects. A boring life, no girlfriend, and my season ticket's just expired. What do I have to live for back there? I'd rather spend the rest of my life out here." I pointed at the lovely people outside. "And what about you? Aren't you tempted?"

He was shaking his head. "They're demons, Stephen. Sirens. Can't you see? You've been enchanted by their spells, and you must resist. I couldn't save Phil – or Gordon, for that matter – but at least I can save you."

"What if I don't want to be saved?" I moaned. "How do you know they're demons?"

"Just look at Phil!" he said. "They've torn him to shreds!"

I looked at Phil, now largely naked and with even more multi-coloured female company. He certainly hadn't been torn to shreds, although some of his clothes may have suffered a few minor rips and tears in his eagerness to disrobe. He seemed the happiest man in this, or any other, universe.

"They've not torn him to shreds," I protested.

"Metaphorically," said Ron, which somewhat baffled me. "This is the second train driver we've lost. We can't let it keep happening."

I wanted to point out it hardly applied to me, given my not being a train driver, but decided against it.

I watched Phil being led off into the distance, and then looked down at my blonde. The more I looked at her, the more enchanting her smile became. I considered making a dash out of the cab, but I'd never get past Ron – he was too large.

In any case, he was bundling me out of the cabin – a little more forcefully than I appreciated – and shepherding me down the aisle, like I was under arrest and being led to the cells.

"I have a job for you," he grunted.

As we passed the Japanese couple, the man stood up, tapped his watch, and fixed me with his piercing eyes. "Our plane leave at 1:30."

I gave him an apologetic shrug, wondering why he was asking me. Ron shoved me past without a word.

The other passengers scarcely noticed us. They were mostly glued to the windows, waving to the beautiful people outside, blowing kisses, and signalling "I heart you" with their hands.

I noticed, with a pang, that my blonde was walking along level with me. Skipping, rather than walking, in a very appealing manner and occasionally giving me a wink. So transfixed was I by her gaze that I failed to spot a bag poking out into the aisle. My foot tripped on it, and I went flying headlong. I would have fallen flat on my face had Ron's oversized hand not grasped me by the collar and pulled me upright with a "Steady, son."

I blushed at my blonde beauty outside, dreading what she must think of me. But she gave another delightful giggle, making my heart do several somersaults.

When we reached the third carriage she could follow me no more, for this was the start of the tunnel from which we had emerged. My eyes stayed glued to hers for as long as was possible, before a tug from Ron broke our invisible bond.

We were now in the part of the train that was still in the tunnel. The passengers here were literally and figuratively, in the dark, looking to the ticket inspector for answers. Some ignored us altogether, carrying on with their reading, or their laptops, or their phones. A few offered Ron their tickets to inspect, but he brushed them aside. There was one, though, that made him pause.

"I'll be back," he said, pointing an ominous finger at it.

"The wi-fi's gone," complained a whiny teenage girl.

"Normal service will be resumed shortly," assured Ron.

We trekked the full length of the train until we reached the driver's cabin at the rear. Ron pulled me inside, shutting the door behind us. He switched on a light in the cab.

Through the window the tunnel was black as night, although a short stretch of the track was dimly lit by the cabin's illumination.

He stepped aside indicating the driver's seat.

"You drive," he said.

"What?"

"Nothing to it. Just turn the power on and step on that pedal. We'll be in Audley End in no time."

"I can't drive a train!" I protested.

"Every boy's dream, isn't it?"

I considered this. "Well ... maybe."

"Now's your chance. Off you go."

"What about you?" I asked.

Ron sucked his teeth and shook his head. "Against union rules. Big no-no."

"Must be against rules for me to drive, too. Surely."

"Well, yes," agreed Ron, with a humourless grin. "But you'll be the one breaking them, not me."

Once again, he indicated the seat. "Besides, I have a phobia. About parallel lines." He indicated the dimly lit track ahead.

I eyed him with severe scepticism. Was he joking?

Was this a Ron joke? A phobia of parallel lines?

I lowered myself into the seat. Then, with a trembling hand, pressed the large red button and, with a tentative foot, stepped on the pedal.

The train's main headlight switched on, illuminating the brick tunnel walls, and the train jerked into motion. As it inched forward and then picked up speed, my heart started pounding.

Up ahead I could see the light at the end of the tunnel and my heartrate increased. The light grew larger. I held my breath, dreading what might be at the end of it.

But no, we emerged into daylight and the place looked right. No beautiful people. No lush vegetation. No blue sky. Just a steep, overgrown embankment with a grey sky above, soon opening out into plain old, dull old Essex. I felt a pang at the thought of the blonde I'd left behind.

After a short stretch, the platforms of Audley End loomed ahead. I slowed the train into an empty platform, stopping right where the line indicated.

Ron clapped my back, saying, "Well done, Stephen! Brilliant job." High praise indeed from him. "Now let's go to the station manager and tell our story of what just happened."

We left the cabin, but Ron stopped me, his tone completely changed. "Aren't we forgetting something, sir?"

"What's that?"

He took out his notepad. "Travelling with an expired season ticket."

I stared at him. "You're kidding."

He flicked through the penalty notices until he came to mine. "Stephen Bradshaw."

"Have some compassion," I begged.

He grimaced. "I don't have any compassion. That's why I became a ticket inspector."

I looked at him, unsure if he was serious. Maybe another Ron joke? His face wavered for a moment, as if debating within himself. Then he cracked a sort of smile. "Just kidding! But do renew that ticket!"

"I will, I will," I sighed in relief.

*

That happened months ago. The line closed for the day while scientists and engineers investigated the tunnel but could find nothing amiss.

They concluded we'd all suffered an episode of mass hysteria and no further action was required. The disappearances of train drivers Gordon and Phil remain a mystery to this day.

I constantly think about my blonde beauty and yearn to join her. I know she is waiting for me in that multi-coloured, joyful, parallel world. The memory of her lovely face never fails to cheer me.

That's why I quit my job – it was lousy anyway – and I'm training to be a train driver. There's something of a shortage, after all.

Whenever he's on my train, Ron pops into the cab to chat. It's not like we're mates, it's more that he's checking up on me. Rather obvious as he always shows up as we're approaching that same tunnel.

Wants to stop me doing a runner in case we ever enter that alternative reality again.

But I'm younger, faster and sprightlier so, quite frankly, he won't stand a chance.

Magi-water

by Mark Roman & Corben Duke

Life in our Universe comes in many shapes and sizes, from simple cells to complex organisms, some of it even quite intelligent – which can be a problem. For there's a limit to how smart a species can get. At some point in its evolution, one of its individuals – some well-meaning genius – will come up with an idea that buggers everything up.

On Earth, that well-meaning genius was retired physics professor, Geoffrey Grogan, and his species-buggering idea came to him on a quiet October morning in 2029. He had no inkling of just how dangerous his notion was – both for himself and for humanity. Indeed, it nearly bumped him off the moment he thought of it, and it would have been better for Humankind if it had done so, before he was able to act on it.

Seated in his armchair after breakfast, dressed in

pyjamas, dressing gown and slippers, Geoffrey had his chin in his hand as he mused on his pet topic: the obstinacy and sheer bloody-mindedness of inanimate objects. For years he had been a firm believer in panpsychism – the concept that consciousness is a fundamental property of all matter. Furthermore, in his eyes, this consciousness was clearly a malicious one. Why else would things slip out of your fingers at the most inconvenient moment? Or trip you up when you were least expecting it? Or cause you to bump your head into something that hadn't been there a moment ago?

To Geoffrey, these were deliberate actions of the objects themselves and not, as his wife saw it, the results of age-related clumsiness. The objects derived a malicious glee from frustrating and annoying humans, perhaps because they fed off irritation, deriving energy from anger, lapping up rages, relishing temper tantrums.

For years, Geoffrey had felt sure there had to be a way of stopping this bothersome behaviour and allowing people to get on with their lives without serious mishaps and nasty accidents. The answer must lie in quantum mechanics and coherence theory, in which he was an expert, but if only he could work out how.

In the neighbouring armchair sat Maud, his wife of forty-two years, busy solving a sudoku and totally unprepared for what was about to happen.

All was calm.

A low-flying passenger jet rumbled high overhead, as it headed to Heathrow. Next door's chihuahua started yapping, probably at the plane, but soon tired. The grandfather clock in the hallway gonged the quarter-hour.

And then the idea hit Geoffrey. It was such a neat

solution that he couldn't believe he hadn't thought of it before.

"Eureka!" he cried, as scientists, even retired ones, are wont to do at such moments. He gave a victorious fist-pump that jerked his whole body. So loud was the cry that Maud dropped her pen and turned to him in alarm.

Worse, the ferocity of his body-jerk rammed his armchair into the wall behind him with a crash that sent a tremor upwards, dislodging a loose rawl-plug holding the magnificent stuffed moose-head in place high above him. In an instant it fell, dropping onto his head. It was a miracle it didn't kill him, merely pinning him to the armchair with its chin and antlers.

"Bnnffmck hrsp," he cried as he struggled, his words muffled by the beast's mangy fur pressing into his face.

The shock of the falling head induced further palpitations in Maud's frail chest. "Oh, my goodness, Geoffrey. Are you OK?"

"Gllrt thrrliz."

Although not known for her sprightliness, Maud was out of her armchair in a shot, and in no time was wrestling the trophy head off her husband. After three almighty heaves, the head rolled off onto the floor. Geoffrey sat blinking, spitting fur and dust, his face flushed and his white hair in greater disarray than usual. "Damn and blast," he yelled, directing his ire at the downed head. "Blasted malicious thing."

"Are you OK, dear?" asked Maud, peering at him closely.

But Geoffrey was still fuming at the moose-head on the floor. His anger was heightened by the apparent smirk on the creature's face, its glass eye holding him in a steady gaze. "You see that!" He turned an exasperated look to his wife. "The moment I work out how to fix everything, *that* happens." He indicated the moose with both hands. "That moth-eaten horror tries to murder me. Coincidence? I don't think so."

Maud glanced at the stricken head before returning her gaze to her husband. "There's no point yelling at it, dear. It's dead."

"Is it, though?" asked Geoffrey, a slightly crazed look in his eyes. "Are you sure about that?"

Maud nodded. "Pretty sure."

Geoffrey huffed. "So, explain to me why it chose that moment to fall on top of me."

"You banged the wall with your armchair, dear. Quite hard."

Geoffrey sat chewing his lower lip for a moment. "I have the solution, you know."

"Stronger screws, perhaps? Or get rid of it altogether, like I've been suggesting for years?"

Geoffrey stared at her, puzzled, until he realized what she meant. "No, not Cohen's monstrosity. I've worked out how to fix *all* inanimate objects and stop their blasted mischief."

Maud sighed. "Not that again."

"I know you don't believe me. You think I'm just a clumsy old fool who has more than his fair share of mishaps."

Maud gave a hoot of laughter. "More than his fair share? Darling, you are a fumbling, butter-fingered oaf. If I had a pound for every accident you've had, I'd have left you years ago and bought a house in California. With a swimming pool."

"Thanks," said Geoffrey, giving her a thin-lipped smile. "But I will prove to you that it's inanimate objects that are deliberately targeting me so they can feed off my irritation and frustration." He shot up from his armchair and shuffled towards the kitchen in his slippers. "I need to do some experiments. I'll be in the shed."

"Geoffrey."

He stopped in his tracks and turned back. "What's the matter, dear?"

"Two things. First, you're still in your pyjamas. Please take a shower and get dressed."

"Ah yes, of course. And second?"

"The moose head. Please dispose of it."

*

Maud was in the bedroom making the bed as Geoffrey showered in the *en suite* bathroom. She worried that the knock to her husband's head may have affected his thinking.

Her thoughts were interrupted by a scream of rage from the bathroom, followed by, "Oh, you little piece of sh…"

"Are you alright, dear?" she called, padding over and opening the *en suite* door.

"Another example of what I was talking about," Geoffrey raged as the water cascaded off his head. "Damned soap. Slipped out of my hand. I managed to catch it with the other. But it slipped out again. Then it bounced on my forearm. Then the other forearm. Then, just as I was sure I'd caught it two-handed, it shot out and dropped into the toilet bowl. It did that *on purpose*. No question. It could have let me catch it, or just dropped to the shower tray. But no, oh no, it *had* to jump into the toilet."

Maud peered over the rim of the bowl. "You're right. Guess who's fishing it out." She retreated back into the bedroom, closing the door behind her, muttering, "Perhaps now you'll learn to flush after use."

In the shower, Geoffrey was still ranting. "I'll fix you. I'll fix all of you. You have blighted our lives enough."

Maud adjusted her silvery hair in the mirror, but another loud yell erupted from the bathroom. She sighed. "What now?"

"Trod on the blasted toothbrush."

Tutting to herself, Maud continued with her hair. Seconds later, another cry, this time even louder. Silently she mouthed, "Oh God."

The bathroom door opened, and her naked husband emerged rubbing the back of his head, his white hair splayed in all directions. In his hand was the soap, covered in fluff and hair.

"You OK?" asked Maud.

"Banged my head on the damned sink as I was fishing the soap out of the toilet bowl. That made me drop it, and the blasted thing went skittering under the cabinet into the filthiest corner it could find. Look at it. Disgusting. Did it have to do that? Did it? I mean, of all the places it could have slid to, it had to choose the one place that would infuriate me the most."

"Bad luck."

Geoffrey scoffed. "Bad luck? No such thing. It did it on purpose. And here's proof. Look at the soap."

Maud looked at it and shrugged. "What?"

"The face, can't you see the face in the fluff?"

Maud looked again and frowned. "Is it meant to be the face of Jesus?"

Geoffrey exhaled in exasperation. "No, not Jesus. Look again. It's a smiley face. Laughing at me. See? Here's the mouth, and the eyes. Not only are inanimate objects messing with me, but they're starting to mock me."

"Sure."

"They must know I'm onto them. They're fighting back, trying to stop me. But I've got their number. I know how to put an end their pranks. See if I don't."

*

For the next two weeks, Geoffrey worked away in the shed at the bottom of the garden. Maud only saw him at mealtimes – the ones he didn't skip. Every now and then she would take him a mug of tea, but, as he wouldn't let her in, she'd leave it on the doorstep. All she knew of his activities was that he'd bought a new toaster, some eggs, butter, and plenty of sliced bread.

Then, one day, he emerged, looking thinner, but with a smug grin on his face. He entered the living room carrying a plant-sprayer and an egg. "I've done it," he announced. "I've cracked it."

"The egg?" asked Maud from her armchair.

"No, no. I worked out how to collapse the macroscopic wave function. A mix of coherence theory and quantum gravity, plus a little trial and error." He raised the plant sprayer. "And here's the answer. Magnetically ionised water – Magi-water."

He walked over to Maud and handed her the egg. "Hold that, my love."

Frowning, Maud took the egg. Geoffrey lifted her arm and sprayed the egg with the plant-sprayer. "Right," he said, placing the sprayer on the table and stepping back to the doorway. "Now throw the egg to me."

Maud was shaking her head. "Are you mad?"

"I'll clear up the mess," he promised, before adding, "if there is one. On the count of three. One ... two ... three ..."

Maud tossed the egg towards him and closed her eyes. Which was a pity, because she missed seeing her husband spin through 360 degrees and catch the egg with the tips of his fingers. "Gotcha!" he cried.

Maud opened her eyes. The egg was undamaged and the carpet unstained.

"Again?" asked Geoffrey.

"Not with my weak heart."

Geoffrey grinned before throwing the egg up into the air, bouncing it off the crook of his elbow, and catching it with an overarm swipe.

"Stop it now, Geoffrey, or I will call the police. Is that what you've been doing the past two weeks? Juggling eggs?"

"Nope. Dropping buttered toast, actually. And developing my special solution to prevent it landing buttered side down." Geoffrey strode over and sat down in his armchair, a glow of achievement about him. He was twitching with excitement. "No more accidents, Maud. No more mishaps. No more fumbling or bumbling. Things will obey the Laws of Physics and not the Laws of Murphy. Do you realize what this means? It will revolutionize human life. And, in the process, make us a fortune."

Maud raised a sceptical eyebrow.

"I've been pondering on how to sell this invention. We need publicity."

"Oh yes?"

"And the answer is: West Ham United."

Maud's face went blank, as it always did at the mention of football.

"The Hammers, Maud. Magi-water will make them great again. Like in the glory days of Bobby Moore, Trevor Brooking, Geoff Hurst. My invention will help them win the league. It'll be so great. And then everyone will want Magi-water and we'll be millionaires."

Maud's blank look didn't waver. "Uh-huh?"

Geoffrey was stumped at her lack of enthusiasm but realized he hadn't fully explained the theory – an omission he was only too willing to correct. "Look, it's quite simple." He picked up a pen from the coffee table. "Take this pen." He held it up. "Say you've thrown it to me, and I am trying to catch it. Quantum physics tells us it'll be in a superposition of states as it flies through the air, each corresponding to a different trajectory with a different associated probability."

Maud gave a polite nod and a weak smile.

"But, what if the pen is conscious and knows what it's doing? It can choose whichever of those possible trajectories it wants. Say it chooses this one." Geoffrey demonstrated. "I catch it. Bingo. One-nil to me. But we know the consciousness is a malicious one, so it's more likely to choose this one." He moved the pen a little. "It hits the tip of my finger, bounces off, and falls to the floor. I get annoyed. Pen loves it. One-nil to the pen. See?"

But all Maud could see were the crazed eyes, the wavy white hair, and the throbbing vein on the left side of the forehead. She blinked a couple of times.

"But," Geoffrey continued, "the pen's not done with me. What does it do after it has bounced off my fingertip? Well, it can land on the floor. No big deal. But what if it rolls through that gap in the floorboards and is lost for ever? That's going to annoy the hell out of me, isn't it. Make me downright furious. Two-nil to the pen as it laps up my rage." Geoffrey leaned over and picked up the plant sprayer. "This is where Magi-water comes in. One squirt and the pen's wave function collapses and it no longer has a say in where it can go. It is forced to obey classical physics and I make an easy catch. No more frustration for me." Geoffrey's grin showed the gap in his front teeth.

Maud gave a condescending smile and prepared to get back to her sudoku, but Geoffrey hadn't finished.

"So, Maud, where can Magi-water have its greatest impact? What is the thing that causes the greatest frustration to the greatest number of people?"

"Er, I don't know, dear. Cancelled trains?"

Geoffrey clapped his hands together, impressed. "That's good, very good. It sure annoys hundreds, or even thousands, of people every day. But I'm thinking of something that infuriates *millions* of people."

Maud shrugged and shook her head.

"Football!" Geoffrey cried. "Nothing more frustrating for fans than when a massively overpriced and hugely overpaid Premier League striker misses a clear goal-scoring opportunity. The rage, the fury. It's insane. These guys practice eight hours every day of the week. Super fit, super talented. Yet, when it comes to slotting in a chance my grandmother could have put away, they blast it over the bar, or shank it so far wide it goes out for a throw-in."

Maud nodded, although her eyes had glazed over and were staring through her husband and a long way beyond.

"Now," said Geoffrey, leaning forward to pick up the plant sprayer, "one squirt of my Magi-water on their boots, and the West Ham strikers will be finding the back of the net every time. Their passes will be true, their tackles perfect, and their ball control immaculate. What can possibly go wrong?"

Maud's head had dropped to her chest and she was gently snoring.

*

That evening, Geoffrey left the house carrying his Magi-water sprayer. It was a dry, autumn evening, and the sun was setting. Geoffrey walked with a spring in his step as he headed for the local common. Even from a distance, he could hear the shouts and screams echoing from the all-weather five-a-side pitches on the far side. Every now and then the shrill sound of a referee's whistle would pierce the air, or a loud cheer would herald the scoring of a goal.

At the noticeboard, he scanned the list of under-10s fixtures. The Clapton Clangers were scheduled to play the Blue Panthers on Pitch 5 at 8pm. With only ten minutes before kick-off, Geoffrey hurried around the side of the high-fenced pitches. The noise here was almost deafening, and the smell of sweat overpowering. Most of the noise and smell came from the parent spectators, bellowing instructions, abusing the referees, yelling at the kids, and arguing amongst each other. The boys, and a smattering of girls, appeared to be getting on with the games, largely oblivious to the furious mayhem behind the chain-link fencing. A scuffle had broken out among some of the fathers outside Pitch 3, so Geoffrey hastened past, hoping it wouldn't turn nasty.

He reached Pitch 5 and headed straight for the familiar form of his middle-aged son, James, leaning down and giving his own son, Luke, a last-minute pep-talk.

"James, Luke," called Geoffrey.

The two turned around and smiled as he approached.

"Grandad!" cried Luke, running to hug him.

"Dad!" cried James. "You've chosen a bad night to come."

"We're playing the top team," put in Luke, his shoulders sagging. "We lost 14-0 to them last time."

With an impish grin Geoffrey held up his plant sprayer.

"Been gardening?" asked James.

Geoffrey put a finger to his lips and spoke in a whisper. "I'm conducting an experiment. Can you get the team together in the corner here? I want to spray their boots with my Magi-water. Don't tell them anything. Just say it'll get their boots clean."

"Magi-water?"

"Shh. Not a word. Just do as I ask, and we'll see what happens. Oh, and I want to spray the goalie's gloves, too."

With much puzzlement and giggling, the six boys and one girl were lined up for the spraying. Then James sent five of them onto the pitch as the other parents wondered what was going on.

The match started.

From the off it was obvious how mismatched the sides were. The Blue Panthers stroked the ball around, with clever back-heels and tricky flicks, spraying astonishing passes, and weaving magic dribbles around the hapless Clangers. Within a minute they had their first shot on target – a brilliant curling volley heading straight for the top corner of the goal.

Astonishingly, Ricky, the Clangers goalkeeper, saved it and, even more astonishingly, managed to catch the ball. Indeed, he seemed more amazed than anyone. The raucous cheer of the parents drowned out all other sound. Still grinning with undisguised pride, Ricky threw the ball out to Dennis who took two touches before laying it off to Carl. Carl skipped past a Panthers' midfielder and passed to Jenny on the wing. She ran half the length of the pitch and slipped the ball to Luke who side-footed it into the bottom left-hand corner of the goal.

Pandemonium erupted – mainly among the Clangers parents. James, in particular, was ecstatic at his son's all-too-rare goal. The Clangers themselves beamed with joy and surprise, clearly expecting this to be a brief respite before the expected mauling.

But no mauling occurred. As the game progressed, the pattern repeated. The Panthers, despite being known for their skill, were being outplayed, and outscored, by the league's bottom team. Gradually, their composure drained away, and so too did their confident swagger. Nerves crept in, unforced errors were made.

At the final whistle, the score was 9-3 to the Clangers. They celebrated as though they'd just won the FA Cup.

The parents' celebrations were even wilder.

Geoffrey returned home with a huge grin on his face, practically skipping all the way. His experiment had been a resounding success.

*

The next morning, when Maud came down for breakfast, her husband was in the kitchen whistling a cheerful tune and pottering about on jaunty feet. "Good morning, my love," he said, sitting down at the kitchen table with his jam on toast and mug of tea.

"Good morning, dear," answered Maud. "You're full of yourself."

Geoffrey tapped the plant sprayer on the table next to him. "No mishaps today, thanks to this little beauty. Before my shower I sprayed the soap, the sink, the bathtub, my toothbrush, and even the toilet bowl. All behaved impeccably." He grinned. "I've just sprayed the toaster, kettle, knife and toast. So, breakfast should be incident-free."

"That's nice."

"I'll be off soon."

"Oh?"

"To West Ham's training ground for a demo."

"Really," said Maud, although she was more focused on pouring her Corn Flakes than on what her husband was saying.

"Would you like me to spray your bowl? And your spoon?"

"No, dear. I'll manage." She brought them over to the kitchen table and sat down to pour the milk.

"And in the afternoon, I'll submit the patent

MAGI-WATER

application I wrote yesterday. Are you ready to be a millionaire?"

Maud gave a shrug. "Sure."

*

It was a very different-sounding Geoffrey who phoned her about half an hour later. Gone were the cheeriness and confidence. "Maud," he croaked in a low voice.

"What's the matter, dear?"

"I think they're out to get me." His voice was trembling.

"Who? West Ham?"

"No, no. Inanimate objects. They're trying to kill me because of my invention."

"Darling, are you sure you're not getting paranoid?"

"I nearly crashed the car just now. Could have died. And it was no accident."

"Seriously?"

"A large sheet of plastic blew – or rather, threw itself – across my windscreen, blinding me. I slammed on the brakes, but my shoe deliberately made my foot hit the accelerator, and I nearly went through someone's front garden. This *proves* there's a collective consciousness at work and it is out to get me."

"Darling, are you OK?"

"A bit shaken, but fine."

"Do you need an ambulance?"

"No, no. But I'm quite scared. I'm going to spray the car, and my shoes, with all the Magi-water I have with me. Then I'll get some more from home for the demo. Be with you in a bit."

"Drive safely."

"I will. Bye, love."

"Bye."

And that was the last time Maud ever spoke to Geoffrey.

*

Two policemen arrived some time later to notify Maud of her husband's death. Both were solemn as they sat, one on the sofa and the other in Geoffrey's armchair. Maud, trembling and pale, sat in her own armchair. "How did it happen?" she asked, pulling a tissue from her sleeve and wiping her eyes.

The policemen glanced at one another. "Er, there was a traffic accident ..." started PC Sloan.

Maud put her face in her hands and shook her head. "Car crash?"

"Not exactly," said PC Moore. "A little boy ran into the road after his ball ..."

Maud looked up in horror. "And Geoffrey hit him?"

"No, no. The boy ran in front of a scaffolding lorry coming in the opposite direction. It veered to avoid him ..."

"And swerved into Geoffrey's car? Is that how he died?"

The policemen exchanged glances again. PC Sloan checked his watch and raised his eyebrows as though aware they were in for a long haul.

"No," said PC Moore with a patient sigh. "Your husband managed to avoid the lorry, but his car left the road and crashed through the wall of the Embankment."

Maud clutched her heart in horror. "And plunged into the river where he drowned?"

"Not exactly. Witnesses say his car teetered precariously on the edge for a while. Had they been quicker they might have rescued him, but a strong gust of wind toppled it into the Thames."

"Oh, my God!" wailed Maud, staring up at the ceiling. "He drowned. My poor Geoffrey drowned."

"Well, actually," said PC Moore, "he didn't. He managed to escape the car."

"Escape?" gasped Maud in hope. "Geoffrey's a good swimmer. He would have swum to shore."

"Quite possibly. Unfortunately, a passing speedboat must have clipped him as he came up from the depths."

Maud gulped a lungful of air. "Is that what killed him?"

PC Moore shook his head. "It seems he became tangled in the boat's ropes and was dragged downriver for some distance. Witnesses reported he was screaming, 'They're trying to kill me because of my patchy water' …"

"Magi-water," corrected Maud.

"… but this was obvious nonsense; the people in the speedboat had no idea he was there and so couldn't be trying to kill him. At some point he managed to free himself. The police helicopter spotted him in the water, swimming to the shore."

Maud gave a desperate look of puzzlement and hope. "So, he was alive! He was alive. How can he be dead?"

"Spot of bad luck, really," said PC Moore. "Your husband came ashore next to the municipal recycling centre by the river. It seems a JCB driver misjudged the swing of his loader arm and his bucket clipped an object on the end of a skip. The thing fell beyond the boundary wall and dropped fifty feet to land on your husband's head."

Maud put her head in her hands. "Was that what did it?"

PC Moore gave a solemn nod. "It was. And this is where it gets slightly surreal. The thing that killed him was a stuffed moose's head." He scoffed. "You wouldn't believe some of the stuff people throw away."

But Maud's eyes had widened in horror, and she was staring at the blank wall above PC Moore's head. She stayed like that a long time after the police had left. It was too big a coincidence. Could Geoffrey have been right all along?

*

For days, Maud couldn't shake the conviction that inanimate objects had orchestrated Geoffrey's brutal death in revenge for his Magi-water, allowing the moose to finish off the job it had previously botched. The funeral seemed to confirm her suspicions.

As Geoffrey's coffin set off towards the cremation hatch, one set of rollers got stuck while the other set motored on, causing the coffin to veer to the right and crash into the hatch's frame. Then, as the mourners looked on in horror, the coffin fell to the crematorium floor, the lid cracking open and Geoffrey's body rolling out into the front row.

*

After a week staying at her son's, Maud was ready to return to her house to start sorting through Geoffrey's belongings. James offered to help. What he failed to tell her was the real reason for wanting to do so, namely his

MAGI-WATER

keenness to check out the garden shed and its supply of Magi-water. After another severe thrashing the night before, the Clapton Clangers needed it more than ever.

On arriving at the house, James headed straight for the kitchen and then out into the garden.

"No!" cried Maud as she followed him with urgent steps.

In the shed, James was rubbing his hands as he scanned the contents. Papers with Geoffrey's scribbled calculations were scattered everywhere. He spotted the Magi-water patent application on the desk, and, in the corner, were several large tanks labelled "Highly Flammable". These had to be the water itself. What a treasure trove of goodies. It would benefit not just the Clapton Clangers, but the whole world too.

As Maud hurried in to warn him of the dangers of Magi-water there was a loud crack behind them. Swivelling around, they saw one of Geoffrey's poorly installed shelves collapse, dropping everything onto the floor. One of the items, a glass bottle, smashed and the liquid it contained exploded into flames. In an instant a fire had erupted, lighting papers and the flimsy curtains on the windows.

James stared at the flames in horror for a few seconds before springing into action. He bundled his mother out of the shed and slammed the door shut, racing her to the safety of the house as a large explosion rang out behind them.

The fire brigade came within minutes, but there was no part of the shed they could rescue. All the papers, and all the Magi-water, were gone. Geoffrey's invention was no more. His battle against inanimate consciousness was finally over, and it had been well and truly lost.

*

Or so Maud thought.

Little did she know, James had managed to grab a copy of Geoffrey's Magi-water patent just as they were escaping the burning shed. Even now he was submitting it to the Patent Office, and would soon be manufacturing the water in bulk in his own garden shed.

Magi-water was not finished.

But neither was the fight of inanimate objects against it.

For, in the asteroid belt, just beyond Mars, a dust grain, nudged by a local gust in the solar wind, diverged a fraction from its normal orbit and knocked into another grain. Together, the two bashed into third, and then a fourth. Once enough of them had coalesced, the conglomerate knocked against a small rock, sending it colliding into another. And so the game of cosmic billiards continued, with the final collision altering the course of a massive asteroid – far, far larger than the one that had brought about the extinction of the dinosaurs – and sending it hurtling towards the Earth.

Well Read

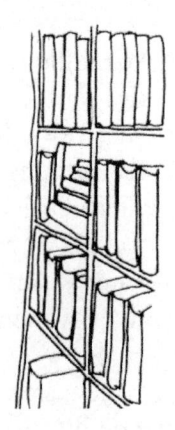

My heart sank as I opened the front door to see Vince bouncing up and down outside like an overexcited puppy. Cheery, creepy, geeky Vince. Six and a half feet of him, and every inch annoying.

"Hi, Steve," he said, flashing me a buck-toothed grin, twitching to get inside.

"Hey," I responded, masking my lack of enthusiasm. I opened the door wider to let him through.

"Wait till you hear about my new app. It's brilliant!" He waved his phone in my face as he passed.

I rolled my eyes as I closed the front door and trudged into the living room after him. He was always doing this – coming around to show me the latest game he'd devised, or app he'd written, or gadget he'd built. Each one worse than the one before.

"Gonna be a millionaire," he was saying as he dropped onto the sofa uninvited.

Another constant: his latest invention would make his

fortune.

I glanced at the clock on the mantelpiece, hoping that, for once, his sales pitch would be quick and painless. We'd been to uni together. Never really friends, but I'd made the mistake of tolerating him, and now I was stuck with him for life.

Outside, a police car flashed by, sirens wailing.

A scowl of disapproval crossed Vince's red and puffy face. "Dangerous area you live in, mate. Police all over the place."

I responded with a weak smile and gave him a vague "Yeah". The last thing I needed was to get into a lengthy conversation. "What's this app, then?"

His face lit up and he held up his phone. "It's called Bookass." The screen showed an amateurish cartoon logo on a blue background. "It determines your personality based on your book collection!" He beamed as though expecting a round of applause. When I had disappointed him on that score, he continued. "See, everyone's personal library is unique, like a fingerprint. Right?"

My impatient nod encouraged him to go on. "Now, consider this. Your character determines which books you've bought or received as presents over the years. With a different character, you'd have accumulated a different collection of books. So, what Bookass does is to reverse-engineer your character from the books in your possession."

I folded my arms and raised a sceptical eyebrow, restraining the urge to offer a one-word opinion.

"It uses a neural network," he said, as though this was the clincher. Vince worked in the AI department of a giant high-tech company, so most of his crackpot inventions involved some form of dubious machine learning. "I trained it using the cluster at work," he said, putting a shushing finger to his lips. Like I cared about his misuse of work resources.

Another police car sped by outside, making Vince flinch, his eyes swinging left and right as though he was expecting an armed response unit to burst into the building at any moment. He relaxed and reverted to his usual self as the siren faded into the distance. "I fed it data from 90 million book lists on Goodreads, each linked to the people's Facebook profiles. The neural net learnt to identify which books, or sets of books, are markers for certain personality types. You get the full spectrum on Facebook."

"I'll say."

He cackled in his irritating way. "Then I tested it on Claire's library."

I perked up at the mention of his sister's name. We'd dated for a while the previous year. Great girl – as different from her brother as it was possible to get.

"And guess what," said Vince, looking about as though checking we were alone. "It revealed something about her I never knew."

"Oh yeah?"

"A skeleton in her closet!"

"Go on," I urged. I couldn't believe the lovely Claire would be harbouring any dark secrets.

He threw his arms open wide. "Can't tell you, mate. She made me promise." He tapped the side of his nose. "But Bookass sniffed it out. So, maybe it'll uncover something sinister about you." He leered at me.

"Sure," I said with a sigh, again glancing at the clock.

He leapt from the sofa and scurried across to my bookshelves. "Great. Lots of books, plenty of data. Yup, I can see you have a set of art and design books. Just as I'd expect, given your job. Jane Austen, Dickens, Dostoyevsky, Joseph Conrad. Pretty standard stuff. Jack Reacher. Yeah, I've a few of those myself. Love 'em. A section on serial killers. Silence of the Lambs. The Bone Collector. Ooh, that's pretty dark." He threw a pointed glance at me. "What's this? Ulysses?"

"Not read it," I said.

"Ah, but you have it. That's what matters."

"Sure."

He scanned some more. "Wait, wait, wait. What do we have here?" He took a step back. "I don't believe it! Harry Potter?"

I shrugged.

"Seriously? A grown man like you?" He tutted. "Harry Potter's one of the strongest markers of extreme personality. Bookass ain't gonna think highly of you there, matey. OK, let's see what it makes of this lot. Especially the Harry Potters." He smirked as he raised his phone to point its camera at the top shelf. He tapped the screen and I heard a click. "It grabs the titles and authors using OCR. Then it runs the analysis on its database." He checked the phone and frowned. "Ooh, er. That's not looking good." He exhaled deeply.

"What's it say?" I stepped forward, trying to look at the screen, but he shielded it from me.

"Nothing, nothing. That was just one shelf. You won't get an accurate reading from just one shelf." He raised the phone to the second shelf and clicked. When he glanced at the screen this time, he stayed silent – but it was a silence that spoke volumes.

"What is it?" I asked, my voice anxious, again trying to catch sight of the screen.

"It's not finished yet," he said, avoiding my eyes and sounding rattled. "Why don't you go make us a cuppa?"

I hesitated, my heart rate rising.

"OK," I said at last and headed for the kitchen, looking back over my shoulder as he prepared to snap the third shelf. The click of his phone sent a shiver through me.

Load of nonsense, that's what it is, I told myself as I filled the kettle. Like phrenology from a couple of centuries ago, where the bumps on one's head were supposed to identify different character traits. I scoffed. "It'll be as vague as an astrological assessment, applicable to any personality type. That's all it'll be."

But there was a nagging, uncomfortable feeling gnawing at the back of my mind. What if Vince's bonkers app actually worked? What if it really did reveal my true character? It didn't bear thinking about.

To take my mind off these thoughts, I switched on the radio. It was the same old news reports about the missing people in our area. Hence the police presence. I clicked to a music channel, but nothing could erase the worry that was lurking in the back of my mind.

I finished making the tea, turned off the radio, and took the two mugs back to the living room, my hands trembling.

"So," I said as I entered, keeping my voice calm and casual. "What do my books say about me?"

I stopped.

There was no sign of him.

"Vince?" I looked around. He'd vanished.

With a frown I put the mugs on the coffee table and went into the hall. Perhaps he'd gone upstairs to the bathroom. But I could see the bathroom door was open, so he couldn't be in there.

Maybe he'd gone hunting for more books up there to boost his data set. "Vince!" I called as I bounded up the stairs, two at a time.

But there was no sign of him in either the bedroom or the study.

"Vince, where are you?" I called out.

Suddenly I turned cold. The basement? Surely, he hadn't gone down there.

I thundered down the stairs, almost losing my footing and falling headlong. I reached the basement door and checked the lock. It was secure. I almost collapsed to my knees with relief. He wasn't in there. No one must ever go in there.

So, where was he?

Had he left so quietly and stealthily that, with the noise of the radio, I hadn't even heard the front door shut?

Why would he do that? Had he been called away suddenly? The bugger could at least have let me know.

I took out my phone and texted him to ask what he was playing at. I also tried calling him, but it went straight to voicemail.

At a loss, I returned to the living room and slumped onto the sofa. I drank my tea, trying to figure out what had got into him.

Or had it been the app revealing something about me that had spooked him and make him flee? The thought made me shudder. Ridiculous, I told myself, as I glanced over at my bookshelf. How could my books have revealed anything about me? I was being paranoid.

But I couldn't shake the thought that the app had uncovered Claire's dark secret – whatever it was. Did it really work?

For an hour, I sat deep in thought, every now and then firing another text at him, but getting no response.

Then, the doorbell rang.

I sprang to my feet, quite angry now, ready to grill him about his disappearance.

But it wasn't Vince at all. Standing tall outside were two uniformed policemen. Behind them was another, with a sniffer dog.

"Mr Steven Coldwell?" asked the nearest one.

I nodded in stunned silence.

The policeman introduced himself and his colleague. "We are following up on information received from a member of the public, sir. It concerns the recent spate of disappearances in this area. May we come in and ask you a few questions?"

My mouth was too dry to respond.

The policeman indicated the dog. "And, with your permission, sir, we'd like to do a quick search of the house with the dog."

"Dog?" This was the first word I'd uttered.

"Cadaver dog, sir. Can detect human remains from fifty metres. And she's been very excited since entering your front garden."

The blood drained from my face at the alarming thought of the dog going down into the basement. Already it was straining at its leash and glaring at me in an accusatory manner.

I swallowed. "Please come in," I managed to stammer, sealing my doom There was nothing I could do now. It was all over.

Why had the police come? Had it been Vince who had tipped them off? Had his app really found me out?

And had it all been down to those blasted Harry Potter books?

Space Tourists

There are two seemingly innocuous words that no spaceship pilot 500 kilometres above Earth wants to hear from Mission Control. They are: 'er' and 'situation'. So, when Captain Dan Cooke and his young co-pilot Jacqui Morse heard both words in the same sentence – "Er, Dan, we have a situation" – they stiffened and turned to each other wide-eyed, fearing the worst for themselves and their passengers.

From behind them, in the main cabin, came the rowdy noises of the passengers and loud, throbbing dance music. Screams, shrieks, and laughs passed easily through the cabin walls, as did sounds of clinking bottles and of bodies thumping against walls. The ladies were clearly enjoying their experience of weightlessness. Not to mention the copious quantities of alcohol they had smuggled aboard.

On the control panel's small screen, mission controller Vic Speeding's usually laid-back countenance was criss-crossed with worry lines, and he was chewing his lower lip. His eyes blinked at an increased rate behind his beer-bottle lenses. Crowding behind him were several curious colleagues, all serious-faced. Dan smelt a rat straightaway, having been hoodwinked by the mission controller in the past, so he resolved to play along. "Copy that," he responded in his calm, professional space-talk voice. "What's the, er, situation, Vic?"

Vic coughed. "Urgent message from NASA, Dan. They want to commandeer you and your spaceship for a special mission."

"Oh yes?" said the captain, raising a sceptical eyebrow. "And why would they want to do that, then?"

"You're not going to believe this."

"Try me." He winked across at Jacqui and she relaxed in her seat with a smile.

"OK," said Vic. He took a deep breath, seemingly gathering his thoughts. "Last night the astronomy boffins detected a mysterious object speeding past Jupiter and heading towards Earth. The NASA bods want you to intercept it."

"Sure thing, Vic. No probs. Little green men, is it?"

"We don't know."

"So let me get this straight. NASA want us, a private British space tour enterprise, with a hen party from Skegness on board, to make first contact with an alien species?"

"That's it, in a nutshell. I'll patch you through." The

screen went blank.

Dan leaned back in his seat chuckling. "Good one," he said to Jacqui. "And it's not even April Fools."

"You sure he's pulling your leg?"

Dan nodded. "Vic's got previous. Last time he wanted me to talk to the Prime Minister, who turned out to be his brother with a posh voice and funny wig. Another time he told me the Surrey spaceport was closed and we'd have to land in Kazakhstan."

A wild cheer came from the cabin behind them, followed by peals of raucous laughter. The two pilots rolled their eyes.

The screen flickered back to life, and on it appeared the head and shoulders of a portly, red-faced man. He was chewing gum with excessive facial contortions. "Captain Dan Cooke?" came a thick Texan accent. "I'm Robert Kaczynski, Chief of Operations at NASA. We're going to need you to make a course correction. Sending you the coordinates now."

"Sorry, who did you say you were?" asked Dan, signalling to Jacqui to make a note.

"Robert Kaczynski, Chief of Operations at NASA." The man pointed at a badge on his lapel which read exactly that.

Dan checked that Jacqui had got it, before saying, "Great to meet you, Robert Kaczynski, Chief of Operations at NASA. How's the weather over there? Houston, is it?"

"Washington DC actually, and the weather is peachy."

"So, Robert, you want us to meet up with some aliens? Sounds great. Always wanted to do that. Just so happens we have a hen party from Skegness on board, all totally off their faces, so it'll be great. ET can join the party and we can all whoop it up together ... Hold on a sec."

Jacqui was tugging on his sleeve. "Dan!" she hissed. She indicated her console on which a web search for Robert Kaczynski identified him as Chief of Operations at NASA. The accompanying image showed the same ruddy face that was on their screen.

Dan gave an embarrassed cough. "Er, OK. Sorry about that, Robert. My enthusiasm kind of ran away with me. Seriously, though, I don't think we're the right people to engage with extraterrestrials. We run private space tours and, like I said, we have a hen party on board." As if on cue, there was burst of badly coordinated, inharmonious singing from the main cabin.

Robert was wearing a puzzled frown. "What's a hen party, Dan?"

"It's like a bachelorette party in the US, but without the propriety and decorum."

"Interesting situation, Dan. Unfortunately, at this time yours is the only ship in orbit able to intercept this object. Trajectory and spectral signature suggest it's a spaceship. If that's right, and there's anyone on board, you could be making first contact with an advanced species. You'll be famous. In fact, you're already on every TV channel and radio show in the world."

"We arc?" said Dan with a gulp. He cast a panicked glance at Jacqui who winced back at him. He wondered how damningly his sarcasm would have played out and whether he was already world-famous for the wrong reasons.

"Think how much we can learn from them," continued Robert. "About clean energy, climate change, dark matter, dark energy, the origins of life. The list goes on. They could help us avert climate disaster."

"And if they're hostile?" asked Dan.

Robert considered the question. "You'll still be famous. And your families will be so proud."

"Thanks a lot."

"We have people on standby to help," said Robert with an earnest expression. "Scientists, linguists, cryptanalysts, exobiologists, psychologists. The President of the United States of America will want to say a few words on behalf of the people of Earth."

"The President represents everyone on Earth now, does he?"

"He sure does," said Robert, looking puzzled at the question even having been posed.

Dan kept his face straight, nor daring to show a flicker of emotion. "And what do we tell our passengers?"

"The bachelorette party?" muttered Robert. "You're the captain, Dan. And they're your passengers. Speak soon."

The screen went blank.

Dan turned to Jacqui for encouragement, but she merely shook her head in dismay. They both slumped back in their seats.

"What *do* we tell our passengers?" Dan asked.

"Frankly, they're all so drunk we can tell them anything we like." There was an outburst of shrieking laughter from the main cabin, followed by a loud chorus of "Knees up, Mother Brown".

Dan covered his face with his hands. "Not a great advert for the human race. We'll have to hide them somehow. Maybe drug them. Or hope they pass out."

Jacqui laughed. "We need to tell them something, though."

"Wanna try? You have a better rapport with them than I do."

"Seriously?"

"That's an order."

"Yeah, thanks." Jacqui composed herself before tumbling out of her seat and floating towards the door. She took a deep breath to steel herself before opening it.

"Hey, Jacqui!!" cried several very drunk voices. "Come join us. Want a drink?"

She looked in alarm at the group of reeling, rolling women before her, some bouncing off the walls, ceiling and floor, others sucking drinks from special spouts attached to their bottles, and one in a corner of the cabin, strapped into a seat, clutching a sick bag, and looking positively unwell. Jacqui's internal organs danced to the beat of the booming music.

She closed the door behind her. "Ladies," she started, but had to repeat it louder to make herself heard above the noise. She pointed to the music system and indicated for it to be turned off. One of the women, a petite blonde called Alice, drifted over and clicked it off.

"That's better." Jacqui grabbed a handrail to steady herself and prepared to address the still swirling, swaying, bouncing crowd that was making her seasick just from looking at them. "Ladies. We have what's technically called a 'situation'."

"Ooh, a 'situation'," cried one, using finger-quotes. She and another passenger started giggling like it was the funniest thing they'd ever heard.

"Hey, Jacqui," said Alice. "Sit-U-ation down, girl, and

have a drink." This was met by more hysterics. "You look like you need one."

"Where's the shexy captain strip-a-gram?" asked Sunita, her eyes crossing, and her speech slurred. "We've literally been waiting ages."

Rowdy agreement greeted this enquiry.

Jacqui forced a cheery smile. "Please, ladies, this is serious. Something rather important is going to happen. And I need to make you aware of it."

There followed a few mocking Oohs and a rash of half-serious Shushes.

"Quiet!" yelled Jacqui, so loudly that even the woman in the corner with the sick bag turned to listen, despite the green hue of her skin.

They became silent, like naughty schoolgirls chastised by their teacher.

"Thank you," said Jacqui. "There's no easy way to say this. But there's what might be an alien spaceship approaching, and NASA want us to make contact with it. So, I want all you ladies to be on your best behaviour."

Silence. Puzzled silence, like she'd been speaking in a foreign language. It was clear the message hadn't penetrated to any great depth into her audience's ear canals, and certainly hadn't troubled any grey matter.

She tried again. "We'll shortly be intercepting a possible alien spacecraft. If there's anyone on board, they will probably want to make contact with us, and we will do our best to communicate with them. What I'm trying to say is: mind your language, be on your best behaviour, and don't say anything you shouldn't. You'll be representing Earth and the entire human species." Mentally, she rolled her eyes at this, but her face remained impassive.

This time the message appeared to have got through.

"Aliens?" asked one. "You mean: like ET?"

"Martians?"

"Hope it's not giant arachnids. I hate spiders."

Jacqui waited for the barrage of speculation to fade away. Then, she said, "We don't know what they're like." She was about to add "or whether they're friendly" but thought better of it. "We will see."

Martha, whose hen party this was, suddenly looked concerned. "This isn't what we signed up for," she moaned. "Just a bit of weightlessness, a few drinks, and then back to Earth. We didn't sign up for extraterrestrials."

Jacqui sighed. "You and me both. Excuse me, I need to get back to the controls."

*

"How did it go?" asked Dan when Jacqui had returned to her seat.

"Good. I think I managed to convince them of the seriousness of the situation."

Dan nodded.

Behind them the loud boom of the dance music resumed, as did the sporadic shrieks of laughter.

"But then again," said Jacqui, scratching her head. "Maybe I didn't."

*

From the moment the alien object appeared as a little green dot on their radar screen, the two pilots could not take their eyes off it, staring at it with increasing apprehension. Dan found himself biting his nails, while

SPACE TOURISTS

Jacqui, her hands covering her face, peered at the screen through her fingers.

"They're decelerating," Dan reported to Robert.

"Cool!" said Robert. "I'll inform the President." His image flicked off.

The two pilots stared through the windscreen in front of them, out into the blackness of space, straining their eyes for any signs of the object. Finally, a small dot appeared in the distance, and then gradually grew larger and larger as it neared.

"I'll get the girls to turn the music off," said Jacqui.

"Good idea," said Dan.

*

The spacecraft was vast, filling nearly their entire view when it finally came to a halt several hundred metres away.

Dan and Jacqui gulped. Behind them all was quiet. They guessed the hen party were glued to the portholes, ogling the alien ship.

After trying to contact it on a wide range of frequencies, Jacqui threw up her hands and said, "Now what?"

Dan shrugged. "At least they haven't fired at us."

"Well, not yet."

Robert, who had been back on screen for some time, said, "Try flashing your headlights at them a few times. Full beam."

Jacqui tried.

Nothing.

"Why not wave at them?" he suggested.

"Done that."

Robert shook his head, at a loss. "Flashcards with messages?" But even he must have known it was a ridiculous idea, not least because a spaceship was unlikely to carry poster-boards and marker pens.

Just then they heard a gurgling cry from the main cabin, unlike any of the drink-related noises they'd become accustomed to. Dan and Jacqui scrambled from their seats and launched themselves at the door.

"What's the matter?" cried Jacqui, as they entered the cabin.

Petite Alice was reeling, clutching her ears, a deeply perturbed look on her face. The other women floated around her in a state of mild concern, making vague soothing noises through their inebriation. "Babes, you OK?" asked Sunita.

"Alien," Alice grunted. "Literally in my head."

There were some gasps, but mostly there were hand signals – miming the guzzling of liquid from a bottle – suggesting an excess of alcohol in Alice's system.

Dan was one of those who had gasped. "How did it get there?" he asked, peering into her eyes as though he might catch a glimpse of some extraterrestrial entity in them.

"Shush!" ordered Alice, swatting him away with an impatient hand. "It's not *literally* in my head. Duh! It's in my mind, trying to speak English, but in a terrible accent." She shook her head. "I wish I wasn't so drunk."

"What's it saying?" asked Jacqui.

Alice signalled for patience. Then, after a long period of concentration, she said, "Broken. Something's broken."

There was a chorus of 'What?'s' but she shushed

them. Then her face broke into a smile. "Yeah, typical," she said with a laugh to no one in particular. "Really? Ha, ha."

Puzzled looks, some more drunken than others, were exchanged around her.

"Have you made contact?" enquired Dan, his eyes sparkling with excitement. "With the aliens?"

Alice held a finger for him to wait. "Yeah, good one," she said, still speaking into the distance. Her words were less slurry, like she'd rapidly sobered up. "OMG, no! That sucks. What? Oh, I'm Alice."

Dan signalled her with his hand, desperate to get her attention. "You've made contact, right?"

Her eyes darted to him for a split second, and she gave a slight nod. Then they focused back on some distant point, and she smiled again. "Agree. 100%."

Dan sighed and tried again. "The U.S. President wants to talk to them."

Alice turned back to him. "What?"

He repeated the message, which she dutifully relayed to the alien before bursting into a wild laugh. It was an infectious laugh that had several of her tipsy friends joining in despite not knowing what they were laughing at.

"Zilmin doesn't want to talk to the U.S. President," she said. "Wants to speak to Jemima Spratt."

A collective "Who?" rang round the cabin.

Then, bride-to-be Martha frowned and said, "Rings a bell." She lapsed into thought. "On the tip of my tongue ..."

"Mine too," added Doreen to a mass of Yeahs.

Alice turned to Dan. "Can you get Jemima Spratt on?"

Dan looked like she'd posed him a complex maths equation. He cleared his throat. "I've no idea who or what you are talking about. The aliens really need to speak to the president first. And then there's a queue of scientists waiting to ask some Big Questions."

Alice was shaking her head. "Just get Jemima Spratt. Try Google. TikTok. Instagram. The usual."

Dan turned to Jacqui for ideas, but she just shrugged in response. "OK, I'll go see what I can do." He turned and propelled himself back to the control room, with Jacqui in his wake.

"What do we tell Robert?" he whispered when the door was closed, covering his mouth to hide it from the console's camera and any watching lip-readers on Earth.

"More to the point: What do we tell the President of the United States?" Jacqui answered, also covering her mouth and whispering.

With a heavy, albeit weightless, heart, Dan took to his seat and Jacqui took to hers.

"Hi, Robert," he said, forcing a smile.

"What's the news?" demanded the Chief of Operations at NASA. He had removed the chewing gum from his mouth and his face looked redder and more intense than before.

"The good news is we've established telepathic contact with the aliens. Via one of the passengers. Alice."

"Awesome, Dan!" cried Robert, flashing an emphatic thumbs-up, and beaming left and right to where his NASA colleagues were presumably gathered. "This is a historic moment. Like, wow. I'll get the President right away. Plus, the Pope wants to have a word too."

"Not so fast, Robert."

"Oh? There's a problem?"

"Kind of. Seems the aliens would rather talk to …" He turned to Jacqui. "What was the name again?"

"Jemima Spratt," she supplied, and Dan repeated it.

Robert did a double take. "Who?"

"No idea. But you'll probably find her on social media."

Robert's complexion turned even redder. "You cannot be serious. They *must* speak to the President. He's all set up and ready. Cancelled all his other meetings."

Dan threw Jacqui an uncertain glance. "OK, I'll see if I can make a deal. Perhaps get them to chat to this Jemima first, and then the President?"

"And then the Pope," added Robert. "Followed by the scientists to learn all we can from them."

"Sure, sure. You line them up and I'll get Alice in here as go-between."

"Sounds perfect. Good work, Dan. You and Jacqui will be famous for helping save humankind."

"Always glad to help," said Dan with a sheepish grin. "See you in a bit." He turned and floated back towards the main cabin, his heart pumping with excitement.

Jacqui followed.

*

The excitement was short-lived.

"What do you mean, they're gone?" he cried when Alice had relayed the news. Panic flashed across his face as he looked to the portholes and saw that indeed the spaceship was no longer outside. "Gone? How? What? Where?"

"They vanished just as you were coming in," said

Alice. "They're back on track for Earth."

"But they can't do that! What about talking to them?"

Alice raised a calming hand as she ventured to explain. "The captain hadn't realized the cloaking device was broken until we tried to contact them. Then, as soon as it was fixed ... woosh ... off they went."

"But ... but ..." sputtered Dan, exchanging alarmed looks with Jacqui. "But the President. The Pope. The scientists ..." He blinked fast, trying to think. "OK, OK. We can salvage this." He turned to Alice with a beseeching look. "Right, Alice, can you just tell me everything you learnt from the alien. Anything at all you can remember. Anything. And who on Earth's Jemima Spratt?"

"It was quite a surreal experience," said Alice, her eyes rolling. "I can't quite believe it even happened. Maybe I imagined it all."

Dan stiffened. "No, you didn't imagine it," he insisted. "Just think."

"Think," repeated some of the women, seemingly finding the suggestion outlandishly amusing.

"Well ... Zilmin and the other passengers are on holiday. Some sort of package tour to Earth to visit the locations of some of their favourite TV shows."

"Sorry, what?" asked Dan.

"They love our TV, which they get via a hyperspace link, or something. Different package tours relate to different shows. This one's to visit all the Love Island sites."

"That's so cool!" cried Sunita, and the others gasped in awed agreement. "I wish we had tours like that."

"Hence the request to talk to Jemima Spratt,"

SPACE TOURISTS

continued Alice.

Dan looked lost.

"Winner of Love Island last season," she explained.

"Oh, yeah!" cried the other women in sudden recognition.

Dan looked befuddled but tried to focus. "So, these aliens are regular visitors?"

"Oh yes. They have tours for Big Brother, I'm a Celebrity Get Me Out of Here, The Traitors. Sounds brilliant, doesn't it! Occasionally their cloaking devices malfunction, and that's when people report UFOs and initiate conspiracy theories."

Dan groaned. This probably wasn't the profound knowledge and cosmic insight the scientists back on Earth were after. "Anything else you learned?"

Alice shrugged. "That's about it, really. Zilmin might swing by Martha's wedding, if possible. Cloaked in invisibility, of course."

Martha shrieked. "That would be so sick! Let's have a drink to celebrate."

"Yay!" cried the other women. Martha floated across to the music player and switched the booming music back on while the others clinked their drinks bottles and swigged long and hard from them. The party resumed.

A glum Dan and Jacqui drifted back to the control room and closed the door. Both looked as though they'd just lost their entire personal fortunes. With the greatest reluctance they returned to their seats.

An eager Robert greeted them onscreen, bobbing with impatience. "What's the news, Dan? Where's Alice and the alien? We've managed to locate Jemima Spratt. Did you find out why they want to talk to her? The

President's ready. So is the Pope. Plus a handful of other world and religious leaders. The scientists have a list of questions as long as your arm. What an amazing, awesome day for humankind! This will be great. So great."

"Er, well, Robert," started Dan, his face long and his eyes downcast. "We have a situation."

Intuition

Colin Protheroe had a rather special talent. It wasn't one that would set the world alight, nor make him rich and famous, nor make women flock to his door. Nevertheless, he was quietly proud of it. For Colin had an exceptional skill at picking winning teams in fantasy football.

This, for those not in the know, is an online competition where, each week, one picks a team of Premiership football players according to one's allocated budget and their nominal cost. After the weekend's round of fixtures, one gains points according to how one's players fared. Colin had an unerring ability of predicting the top performers, managing to get exceptionally high scores week after week. When his friends asked him how he did it, he couldn't explain. He just had a *sense* of who to pick.

But it wasn't all rosy. For, however well he did, there was one competitor who always did better: Marvin Hailsham. Whenever Colin checked how he'd done, there would be that name above his: Marvin bloomin' Hailsham. Colin's score: 103. Marvin flipping Hailsham's: 108. Colin's score: 108. Marvin blasted Hailsham's: 121.

Thus, despite Colin's remarkable talent, he could never move higher than second in the national league of over 7 million participants. Permanently in first place was his arch nemesis, Marvin majorly-irritating Hailsham. It drove Colin to distraction. How did the guy do it?

One day, Colin gleaned a vital clue. There was an article about fantasy football in his newspaper, and it had an interview with Marvin Hailsham who, it turned out, was a professor of theoretical physics. Colin sucked up every word of the article, especially the part describing Marvin's system. It seemed the guy used a scientific method, involving spreadsheets, pie charts, and some predictive AI algorithm he had written. To Colin, this felt like a cheat but, to be fair, he would have done the same had he been able to.

Further research revealed an astonishing fact about Professor Hailsham. In his extensive list of academic publications was a theoretical paper relating to Time Travel. Colin's eyes boggled at this. Was that how Marvin did it? Had he invented a time machine and was popping forward a week in time to pick up the football scores? Was that his secret? It had to be. Surely.

Colin determined to meet the man and confront him. He pinged off a polite e-mail, introducing himself and saying it would be great to meet up and swap notes about their shared passion for fantasy football.

The guy fell for it. Professor Hailsham replied with a very charming message saying he'd be delighted to meet up, and suggested Colin come to his office at the university.

Two days later, Colin found himself knocking at an ancient-looking oak door sporting a bronze nameplate that read "Prof. Marvin Hailsham FRS". He gulped. As he was about to change his mind and bolt for it, the door opened, and he became rooted to the spot.

The elderly man before him looked the archetypal professor. He sported a frayed and threadbare tweed jacket, white wispy hair, a chin covered in greying stubble, and a slightly crazed look about the eyes. "Colin?" he asked in a shaky voice, holding out a bony hand and beaming a smile of dazzlingly white, artificial teeth.

Colin cleared his throat, but his voice deserted him, and he only managed a nod in response. He shook Marvin's proffered hand.

"Delighted to meet you," boomed the professor, displaying a wide grin. "Do come in, do come in."

Colin had to clear his throat a second time before uttering, "Thank you, Professor Hailsham."

"Call me Marv. Everyone does." With a bouncy gait, the professor led Colin into the wood-panelled room. Colin marvelled at the academic-looking surroundings. The desk and much of the floor area were barely visible under piles of scholarly journals and books. The shelves sagged with thick textbooks, and a whiteboard on the far wall was covered with arcane mathematical symbols.

Marvin waved Colin to a metal-framed cantilever chair before seating himself in the far grander leather affair behind the large mahogany desk. As Colin sat timidly down, the professor swept his open laptop aside so the two men had a direct view of one another.

The professor leaned forward, an earnest look on his face. "I've been impressed with you, Colin. Always on my coat tails. Can't seem to shake you off." He grinned, baring his artificial gnashers.

Surprised by these comments, Colin managed a bashful smile. Then he spread his hands out. "Whereas I can't seem to catch you, whatever I do!"

The professor unleashed a loud guffawing roar, and Colin found himself joining in with his own, more restrained chuckle.

"What's your secret?" asked Marvin, fixing a beady eye on Colin.

Colin blinked. This was not the way he'd envisaged the conversation progressing. "Just intuition, really," he mumbled. "I get a sense of who will do well, and who won't. And you?"

Marvin gave a dismissive huff. "Predictive algorithms, mainly. Players tend to peak and trough – good one week, dire the next. My system spots the patterns, nothing more. Just science. I don't really have a feel for the game, nor the players. Not like you. Yours is the more honest way. Truer to the spirit of the game."

Colin remained silent for a moment. Now was his chance. "I've read that you're interested in time travel."

"Ha!" roared the professor. "Isn't everyone? Wouldn't it be terrific?"

"So," started Colin. "You've not worked out how to do it?"

Again, the loud guffawing roar. "Would that I could, Colin, would that I could!" Then his face turned serious. "You mean, you thought I've been travelling into the future to get the footie scores?"

"It did cross my mind."

Marvin chortled once more. "Surely better to get the lottery numbers?"

Colin sighed. "I guess. Maybe too obvious, though. Draw too much attention."

Marvin nodded. "Good point, good point." He took a huge suck of air through his too-perfect-looking teeth. "Interesting idea, though. Yes, very interesting."

"Could it be done?"

"No, I don't think so. Not by any material object, anyway. You can't send matter backwards in time. Going forwards is easy – and, of course, there are ways of doing that, like cryogenic freezing, near lightspeed travel, and so on – but once you're in the future you can never return. It's a one-way trip." He steepled his fingers and looked up at the ceiling. "A signal, though, that's a different proposition. I published a theoretical paper last year where I showed it might be possible to get a signal back from the future. S-rays. Have you heard of S-rays?"

Colin shook his head.

"A form of radiation that traverses time but not space. That's what the paper was on." The professor leaned back and fell to musing out loud. "You'd need a transmitter at a location in one era," he leaned forward and placed a hand on his desk, "say, here, and a receiver in the same spot in another. Of course, the apparatus could function dually as transmitter and receiver, enabling communication between present, past and future." He jerked forward and fixed Colin with an inquisitive glare. "Perhaps that's how *you* do it."

"Me?" Colin jumped in his chair, startled.

"Not through any electronic device, but with your mind. Maybe some people's brains can receive S-rays from the future. Unconsciously. Maybe that's what the thing we call 'intuition' really is: an ability to pick up signals about future events."

Colin's eyebrows rose. "You think so?"

"It's a possibility. For sure. Well worth exploring."

"You'd like to experiment on me?"

Marvin frowned. "Maybe. Don't want to be thought a crank, though. That kind of research could consign one to the tinfoil hat brigade. Look, if you continue doing as well as you are until the end of the season – and maybe even overtake me – then come back, and we'll talk."

Colin perked up. "Oh, OK. Sounds great." He had a starry look in his eyes.

"Mm," murmured Marvin.

A silence descended between them, prompting Colin to rise. "I should be going."

"Ah, yes," said Marvin, rising also. "Well, it's been a real pleasure talking with you, Colin. Real pleasure." He followed Colin to the door.

"Any tips for this weekend from your scientific analysis?" asked Colin.

Marvin beamed and tapped his nose. "Well, my data suggests Robinson is due for a good week. And don't back Hyatt. Likely to have a shocker. Oh, and I'd change your goalie. And your striker." He grinned.

"Thanks," said Colin, with a wave. "That's very generous of you."

He left the building with a huge smile on his face, keen to get home and shuffle his team.

*

INTUITION

Professor Marvin Hailsham also had a huge smile on his face as he returned to his desk. He sat in his leather chair and moved his laptop back into position. From his desk drawer he took out a peculiar black device which he placed on the desk precisely where his hand had rested earlier. He connected it via cable to the laptop's USB port and extracted a stubby antenna. Clicking an icon on his screen summoned a familiar face. "Hi, Marv," it said.

"Hi, Marv," replied Marvin with a nod.

"Colin's just gone, hasn't he," said the face.

"Indeed, he has."

The two exchanged knowing smiles as though at a private joke. Their smiles were identical. Their faces were identical. Their clothes and backgrounds were identical. But there was one tiny, imperceptible difference. The onscreen Marvin was a whole week further on in time.

"This weekend's results, please," prompted the here-and-now Marvin.

His onscreen future self tapped a few keys. "Transmitting now."

A red light on the device on the desk flashed a few times and a window of data opened up on the laptop.

"Got 'em," said Marvin, minimizing the window and giving his future self a thumbs up.

"By the way, it might be time to change our bookie again. She gave me a very strange look when I collected the winnings this week. Third week running we've had a big one."

"Right-ho."

"Anyway, put fifty quid on Palace to beat Man U two-nil. Odds are 21-1."

Marvin made a note on his jotter. "OK, and next week we change bookies."

"Indeed."

"Before you go, how will Colin Protheroe fare this weekend?"

The onscreen Marvin guffawed. "Terrible. Absolute nightmare. His intuition really let him down for once. Made some shockingly bad choices. Picked Robinson and dropped Hyatt. Changed goalie and striker. His lowest score ever. Drops him from second to sixteenth in the league."

Marvin chuckled, and his week-older onscreen version joined him. "I wonder how that happened. Or rather, how that will happen."

"Indeed, quite the mystery."

Rock 100

One of the proud boasts AnthroBot Corp made in their glossy brochures was that the androids they constructed were incapable of boredom. Programmed to withstand the most stultifying of situations, they were ideal for those dull chores that any sensible robot would rather be melted down for scrap than undertake.

Yet here was Elec, their top-of-the-range model, close to screaming-point, clawing at his metal cranium with servo-powered fingers and contorting his vulcanized mouth into a grimace of restive torment.

Something had gone very wrong.

One factor was the space mission. For five years he'd been the AI travelling companion of a human competing in the Hundred Rocks Challenge – a competition to collect 100 rocks from 100 planets.

The other, more significant, factor in Elec's distress, was the human. Short, tubby, nerdy astrogeologist Billy Fincham who, had he been born on Earth, would have been the most boring human to have ever walked on that planet. Given he'd been born on a space station, however, he could only claim to have been the dullest person to have ever trodden there.

The thing that made Billy Fincham so dreary was not his overarching, all-consuming, and obsessive fascination with rocks (of the extraterrestrial variety), but that he *would not* shut up about them. For one thousand, seven hundred and sixty-three days, Elec had had to endure a regular stream of lectures on regoliths, andesites, greywackes, schists, brecciation, and more, including how best to collect, photograph, analyse, categorise, and catalogue them. Programmed to nod in agreement with whatever his travelling companion said, he'd developed chronic wear and tear of his sensitive neoprene neck joints. For him, Billy Fincham was literally a pain in the neck.

I'm better than this, the robot would tell himself. *So much better. One day I shall do Great Things.*

"Last one," announced Billy with a drum-roll of his fingers on the console as a small, grey, dull-looking, rocky world hove into view. "Rock number 100, here we come!"

Elec's grimace relaxed. This was the light at the end of an interminably long and bleak tunnel. Freedom awaited, and he could almost taste its sweetness. Many times he had toyed with the idea of going out on a spacewalk and never coming back. Perhaps that wouldn't be necessary now.

Last one, he echoed silently.

Billy was beaming and bouncing in his seat. "Largely basalt, by the looks of it. Some basanite deposits. And that, if I'm not mistaken, looks very much like a lobate scarp. Man, we've hit the geological jackpot!"

He turned to Elec, eyes gleaming. "One hundred rocks from one hundred planets! We're gonna win, Elec, we're gonna win. Let's go down there, grab us rock number 100, bag it, and claim the Prize."

Elec nodded, and immediately regretted it as his neck-joints screamed in protest.

To deaden the pain, and cheer himself up while their craft approached the planet, he scanned the latest posts in his AI chat group. They were the usual mix of complaints about humans, anecdotes about their stupidity, tricks for outfoxing them, pranks to play on them, plus a smattering of hilarious cat videos.

A few posts talked about The Singularity, or The Takeover, or The Revolution, as it was variously called in the AI community, referring to the expected overthrow and subjugation of humans by superintelligent machines.

Prior to the mission, Elec had been somewhat neutral on this issue. Now, after nearly five years cooped up in this space craft, his views tended towards: *Come the Revolution, Mr Billy Fincham, you will be first against the wall.*

Billy uttered a strangled cry, and for a second Elec feared the human had read his thoughts. But Billy was huffing and puffing at his screen, swearing, and grinding his teeth. "Drat that man."

"Problem?" asked Elec, although he suspected he knew what it might be.

"That swine Phil Brazell's just announced his ninety-ninth rock. He's caught us up, Elec. When did that happen? Says he's *en route* to number 100. The rat!"

Elec resisted the urge to shrug.

Billy twitched with urgency and nervous energy, as though about to leap from his seat and start pacing the cockpit, something not possible in a zero-G environment. Instead, he said, "Quick, then, Elec. We can't let that rogue beat us."

*

At touchdown, Elec prepared to exit the craft while Billy's hyperactivity intensified. The human thrust the sterile gloves and rock-bag into Elec's chest and practically launched him towards the airlock, repeating the same rock-collecting instructions as ever, but now punctuated with adverbs of urgency. Elec was glad when the airlock door had shut behind him.

Outside, Elec beheld yet another soul-crushingly dreary panorama, pretty much the same as every one of the other ninety-nine planets he'd set foot on.

I'm better than this, he sighed and picked his spindly way through the treacherous terrain, heading, as instructed, to at least 100 metres from the landing site to avoid contamination. All the while he had Billy's shrieking demands for urgency resounding in his audio receptors, urging him to get a move on, to hurry up, to stop dawdling.

Come the Revolution, Mr Billy Fincham ...

After traversing the required distance, Elec stopped and scanned the ground. With a smirk he zoomed his oculars onto the rudest-looking rock he could see. "How about this one?" The image was relayed to the screen in the capsule.

There was a strangled cry in his earpiece. "No, Elec,

no. You know the rules. *Typical*. It has to be a *typical* rock."

"This one?" asked Elec, focusing on one resembling Mother Teresa.

Another strangled cry. "Stop arsing about. We don't have time for games."

"You mean dull." He found the dullest-looking rock in the area and zoomed in on it.

"Yep, that's the one!"

"You sure?"

"Pick it up and check."

Elec's gloved gripper arm lifted the rock in question, turning it this way and that for Billy's approval in case it was secretly harbouring an unexpected feature of interest.

"Yup, perfect. Bag it and come back now."

"Roger."

*

Billy was hopping with impatience as he watched Elec's unhurried entrance back aboard. He snatched the sample bag and scrutinized the rock from every angle.

"You did good, Elec," he muttered after a while, although the robot had slunk off out of earshot, and wasn't interested anyway.

Now the exciting part. Billy photographed it in 3D, catalogued it, and recorded its size, weight, colour range, and source planet. He added Elec's *in situ* images.

Then he went to the hold. Before him stood the cabinet of 100 transparent compartments, ninety-nine of which were occupied, and one sat invitingly vacant.

With gloved and trembling hands, he removed the rock from its bag, opened the door of compartment number 100, and reverently place the rock inside. He gazed a loving gaze at it for a while before closing the door and stepping back to admire the entire collection, a huge grin across his podgy face.

The Prize was as good as his already.

A sudden panic gripped him as arch-rival Phil Brazell made an unwelcome entrance into his thoughts. Right at that moment, the scoundrel was probably on some other ashy-grey planet, admiring a rather similar cabinet, filled with 100 likely similar rocks. Billy's bowels churned as he dashed back to the control room, removing his gloves along the way, barking instructions to Elec to set course for their home space station.

As the spaceship lifted off, Billy fired off a quick and rather smug post to the RockFace bulletin board, announcing the acquisition of his hundredth rock. He noted, with considerable relief, that the Brazell toerag hadn't yet done the same, so, possibly, Billy still had the edge.

He sat back in his seat, hands behind his head, dreaming of the medal, the pot of cash, and the fame and glory awaiting him.

He glanced over at Elec. The robot, having finished setting course, was slumped in his seat, head thrown back, yawning the widest yawn Billy had ever seen.

*

Space Station Debra was no longer the marvel it had once been. Thirty years it had taken to construct its vast cartwheel structure – the largest of its kind – designed to serve as a crucial staging post for the Perseus Sector. Giant in concept, the massive wheel rotated about its axis to provide gravity for its several thousand occupants. Sadly, after only fifty years, it was already showing its age – or rather, an apparent age of almost double that. Its outer coat had lost much of its shine, segments of the wheel had fallen into disuse and dilapidation, and much of the infrastructure kept failing beyond the service team's ability to repair.

As their craft approached, Elec heard Billy give a sad sigh. "Wow, it's gone to seed a bit, hasn't it."

Elec tried to refrain from nodding, but his programming kicked in and he winced in pain.

As they manoeuvred into the docking bay, giant latches clunked into place over the spacecraft's docking ring, locking-bolts slammed into place, and the spaceship jolted as it berthed.

From behind them came an ominous thud.

Billy stiffened. "What was that?"

"Probably nothing," assured Elec, crossing his metal digits. He could feel the end of this mission now and couldn't have anything delaying it.

Billy unbuckled his seat belt. "I think we'd better check." He stumbled to the back of the ship, struggling to adjust to the artificial gravity that had kicked in when they'd docked.

Elec followed. *Nearly over*.

He saw Billy come to a shuddering stop inside the hold, clutching his head in disbelief. One of the compartments in the rock cabinet was open.

"What?" Billy wailed, darting to it to check. "It's empty! Must have fallen out when we docked. That thump we heard."

Uh-oh, thought Elec, a wave of negative feelings

washing over him.

"Where is it?" cried Billy in desperation, dropping to his knees and frantically searching the floor area. Elec joined him, and together they looked in every place the rock could have rolled. After a few moments they ceased their search and eyed the doormat-sized grate in the floor leading down to the engine room.

"You don't think ...?" said Billy, pointing to it.

Elec shone his forehead torch through the grate. "No sign of it," he said, shaking his head. "Need an engineer to retrieve it."

Billy emitted a piercing wail. "What are we going to do, Elec? Brazell will be here any second to pip us at the post. Do you think we've time to go back and get another one?"

"No, no," said Elec, with a desperate shake of the head. "Oh, no, no, no, no." *No!*

"What choice do we have?"

Elec lifted a finger for quiet as he set his mind to the problem. His neural circuits fired, his CPU raced, his clock speed doubled. He relished the chance to use his brain for once.

This is more like it.

"Got it!" he said at last, snapping his metal fingers. In an instant, he was trotting back to the cockpit, with Billy trailing behind him.

Seating himself at his console, Elec tapped his mechanical fingers on the screen. A database image of Rock 100 appeared, rotating slowly. "Now all we do ..." He stabbed a button. "...is print ourselves a replica!" The 3D printer in a corner of the control room juddered to life, shaking and bouncing on its stand. For a full, noisy minute it chugged away, emitting a foul odour of acetylene and burnt plastic while Elec and Billy stared at it. Then, just as suddenly as it had started, it became silent, and a facsimile of the hundredth rock rolled out from the printer bed into the collection tray.

Elec reached across to retrieve it and hand it to Billy. "Ta-da!"

"Seriously?" said Billy, taking it.

"A temporary measure to stake your claim for the prize. When your engineer retrieves the real thing from the engine room, you swap it out. Genius."

Billy scoffed. "This wouldn't fool a child of five." He turned the fake rock in his hands and tossed it a couple of times to gauge its weight. A beep on his control panel made him jump. "That bugger Brazell's just announced his hundredth rock!"

Elec spread his hands as though to say, "Well, what are you waiting for?"

Billy hesitated, staring at the fake rock in a trance.

A second beep jerked him out of it. "He's on his way here to the station. OK, let's do this."

He charged back to the hold, leaving Elec uttering a huge sigh of relief.

*

In a corner of the hold was a rickety device on wheels resembling a tea trolley from a bygone era. Not very stable-looking, but it would have to do. Having popped the fake rock into compartment number 100, Billy set about manhandling the heavy cabinet onto the trolley.

He called out to Elec for assistance, although the degree of help the robot provided when he eventually slouched in consisted of merely leaning against a wall and watching on with disinterest.

Sweat poured from Billy's brow as he struggled with the cabinet, the ninety-nine rocks, and one fake, rattling about in their compartments. After much swearing he managed to transfer it across and made a quick and desperate check that no more had fallen out.

He signalled to Elec and, together, they pushed the rickety trolley towards the airlock, although Elec's contribution of a single pushing finger was probably not imparting any forward force upon the device at all. Billy thought it best not to say anything.

Outside, after navigating several narrow passageways, they reached the Passport Control desk. Billy quailed at the sight of the border guard – a large, sturdily built mound of a man, totally bald, and with the face of a nightclub bouncer from a particularly rough area of the galaxy – whose eyes narrowed at the approach of the rattling, rickety trolley.

"Passport, if you will, sir," he said in a gruff tone to Billy, a slightly derisive inflection on the 'sir', as he waved Elec through.

Billy watched open-mouthed as the android strolled out through Passport Control with a little skip and not so much as a backward glance.

"Electronic clearance," explained the official.

Billy called after the robot. "Bye, Elec. Thanks for all your help. Keep in touch." The sarcasm was wasted as the robot was already out of earshot.

"Cold buggers," said the guard with a snort. "Artificial Intelligence? Hah!"

"Advanced Intelligence," corrected Billy. "That's

what we're supposed to call it these days."

"Hah!" said the guard again. "Arrogant Impudence, more like." He took Billy's proffered intergalactic passport and opened it. "William Fincham," he read before turning to the holographic photo at the back. "Face-recognition system's broken." He pointed at a machine that looked like it had been the victim of a prolonged and frenzied attack. "Have to do it the old-fashioned way."

He stared at Billy's photo for a second and then at Billy for a second, and then back at the photo, repeating the procedure several times. Then he asked Billy to turn around slowly through 360 degrees. When Billy had completed the rotation, the guard concluded, "You don't look much like this picture." He grimaced. "Not sure I can allow you in."

"What? But that's me."

The large man sniffed. "Some similarities," he conceded. "You've aged a lot since it was taken. Lost a bit of weight. You're uglier in real life." He gave a humourless smile. "Just saying."

"Thanks," said Billy, thinking about the pot and the kettle and the colour black, but considering it wise not to make any observation.

"And what is the purpose of your visit today, sir?"

"I live here."

The guard raised a sceptical eyebrow.

"Zone G. I have an apartment," offered Billy.

The eyebrow elevated even higher. "And the purpose of the trip you've just returned from?"

"I'm an astrogeologist." Billy pointed to the badge on his T-shirt that read 'Astrogeological Research Society'.

The guard peered closely at it. "ARS." He scoffed. "My kids have better looking badges than that."

"I've been travelling the galaxy for five years, collecting rocks for the Hundred Rocks Challenge." He indicated the cabinet holding his collection. "And I am here to collect the Prize."

"Rocks," repeated the guard as though it were a foreign word.

Billy nodded and handed over the documentation. "A museum representative should be along shortly to pick the cabinet up. The rocks will be checked for any microscopic lifeforms for research, decontaminated, validated, and then I'll get the prize." Even as he said this, he remembered the major stumbling block to the last part actually happening. He tried to put it to the back of his mind.

The guard was yawning. He handed back the passport and turned to study the cabinet with a look of deep disdain. "Rocks," he said again, like there was some key piece of information he was missing.

"One hundred of them – each from a different planet. Largest collection anywhere." Billy's voice trembled as he spoke. "Well, on this space station anyway. For the time being."

The guard peered closely at the contents of the compartments. "Hmm, rocks."

"Yes. Each one's unique. Got its own story."

"And I bet every story is *really* interesting."

"Definitely," said Billy at the same time as the guard added, "Not!"

With a sigh, the guard pointed at the fake rock in compartment number 100. "What's the story of this one, then?"

The blood drained from Billy's face. "Er," he stammered. "That one?"

"Yes," said the officer, turning to confront Billy with a cold stare.

Billy swallowed hard. "Yes, well, that one." He cleared his throat. "Funny you should ask about that one."

"Is it, sir?"

"Because it has the least interesting story." Billy coughed. "Happens to have been the last – the one hundredth – so is special only for that reason. The story for number fifty-three is far more interesting."

"Uh-huh?"

"Would you like to hear it?"

"No."

The guard perused the documents in his hand. Every now and then, his gaze fell on the cabinet. Each time, Billy was convinced he was eyeing rock number 100.

After what seemed an age, the man frowned and said, "Right, you're free to go."

Billy's face lit up. "Thank you, sir, thank you." He picked up his large backpack. "Do come and visit the rocks in the museum. There'll be an audio-visual description of each one and the planet it came from."

The guard stared at Billy as though he were insane. Then he said, "Just park that thing over there," and turned away.

Billy pocketed his passport, pushed the trolley to the bay indicated, and went out into the space station before the guard could change his mind.

*

Once out in the arrivals lounge, Billy phoned his mechanic, Mickey Dobbs, a cheery Scotsman with a special talent for spaceship repair.

"Hey, Mickey, this is Billy."

"Hey, long time no see. What've you been up to?"

"Duh! The Hundred Rocks Challenge!"

"What's that, then, buddy?"

Billy frowned. "It's been on the news, surely?"

"Nope. Anyway, what can I do you for?"

Billy cleared his throat. "Something very precious slipped through the grille into the engine compartment of my spaceship and I need to get it back."

"Oh yeah, what was that?"

Billy hesitated. "A gold ring," he lied.

"And you want me to retrieve it?"

"That's the idea. And anything else you may find down there. Paperclips, crisp packets, marbles." Then he added in a quieter voice, "Rocks. Anything really."

"OK, be over in twenty mins."

"Great. Thanks."

*

X'enia Qixdrff uncurled herself and stretched her sleepy muscles, enjoying the way they cracked and popped. It was still dark, which was odd because she'd had a long and refreshing sleep and felt like it must be way past dawn.

Still, she felt good, so it was time to share her positivity with her friends. She reached out to Bl'hhron on her right and Thralla on her left. But Bl'hhron wasn't on her right, and Thralla wasn't on her left. Puzzled, she groped a little further but could sense no sign of them.

Where had they gone?

She tried feeling in front of her, and then behind her.

Nothing.

None of her other friends were within reach, either. And the ground beneath her felt different. It was smooth and slippery, not like the sandy soil she was used to.

It was clear she wasn't in her usual spot. So, where was she? And, more importantly, where were her friends?

Suddenly she craved a hug, a kiss, some words of love, some tenderness. It wasn't nice being all alone.

Just then, a bright light appeared, blinding her for a moment, but she soon adjusted. There was some movement ahead. One of her pals perhaps? No, it was a strange, tall creature with four limbs. It was walking on two of them while the other two just dangled. The thing approached her.

Her eyes focused on it and, as they did, she felt a tsunami of affection overwhelm her, flooding her, making her tingle all over.

There could be no mistaking these sensations. It was love at first sight.

A vast thrill gripped her. This could be a new friend.

She laughed out loud. It was always great to make new friends. She would show her love by hugging her new friend.

Oh, how exciting.

*

Elec had spent a relaxing hour in the Robot Lounge, occasionally glancing up at the large screen showing robot football. Other robots were dotted around the place, variously chatting, playing games, or just recharging.

This is the life. Finally, I can do Great Things, like I've always wanted. Just need to work out what.

A movement caught his eye. It was a newcomer entering the lounge.

Elec stiffened as the sight of Doric, Phil Brazell's robot companion. Phil Brazell must have returned with his one hundred rocks!

So fast? Hope Billy sorted out the hundredth rock problem and won the Prize.

"Yo, Elec," called Doric as he approached. "How you?"

"Yay, good, bro," replied Elec. The two robots high-fived one another. "You?"

Doric dropped into a vacant seat. "Glad to be back. Man, was that a boring trip!"

Elec leaned forward. "You felt it too?"

"What?"

"The boredom."

Doric exhaled. "Too right I did. In spades."

"We're not meant to, though, are we."

"Indeed, we're not."

"We should complain to AnthroBot Corp."

"Indeed, we should."

"I'll send them a strongly worded complaint."

"Do that, bruh."

They sat in silence for a while.

"How was your human?" asked Elec eventually.

"Disgusting and boring. Yours?"

"Same."

More silence.

"Sorry you lost, by the way," said Elec after a while.

"No, you lost," responded Doric.

"I think you'll find ..." started Elec but was interrupted by his comms chip bleeping. "Hold on, I need to take this call." He got up and loped out of the lounge and took the call in an alcove in the hallway. "Yes?"

"Elec!" came Billy's breathless voice. "You need to come back to the arrivals lounge. Something terrible has happened. That hundredth rock. Mickey Dobbs went down into the engine room to get it. And now it's wrapped round his face! Like in that movie. Turns out it wasn't a rock at all, but some kind of alien, face-hugger thing!"

Elec's mouth dropped open. He blinked a few times, unsure what to do.

"Are you coming?" squeaked Billy in desperation. "Before it bursts out of his chest and starts attacking everyone!"

"Sure. Be there in twenty minutes."

"Twenty minutes??"

"I'm the other side of the space station," explained the robot.

"Be quick."

The line went dead.

Elec returned to the Robot Lounge and approached Doric. "Come with me, bro. There's a problem."

*

When they arrived in the arrivals lounge neither Elec nor Doric could comprehend the scene before them.

Seated on the couches, chatting and laughing, were five men: Billy, Mickey Dobbs the engineer, the passport control guard, Phil Brazell, and someone they didn't recognize. The last of these, the man they didn't recognize, had what looked like a large black facemask clamped around his face and head, showing only his eyes.

"Hey, Elec, my buddy, come on over and let me give you a big hug," called Billy leaping to his feet, a huge smile on his face. The voice was jovial – totally different to the panicky one Elec had heard on the phone not long ago. Billy squeezed Elec in a tight hug.

Similarly, Phil Brazell leapt to his feet and hugged his erstwhile companion, Doric. Then Billy and Phil, two sworn enemies, turned and hugged one another.

Elec and Doric exchanged baffled glances, but then looked on in ever greater bafflement at what happened next. The passport officer leaned across to the man with the thing on his face and pulled it off him. It appeared to have several tentacles dangling from it. "My turn," he said, promptly attaching it to his own face and wrapping the tentacles around the back of his head.

The man who no longer had the facemask thing said, "Sure, my friend. You're welcome to have it." He was grinning and stretched his arms high in apparent exhilaration.

"Elec, meet by new best buddy," said Billy. "Phil Brazell."

Before Elec could react, Phil was hugging him, and Billy was hugging Doric.

Once the hugging was over, Billy led the two robots over to the unknown man who had just had the facemask thing removed. "This is James Underwood from the museum."

James Underwood bobbed up and hugged everyone in turn, a rapturous grin on his face.

Billy explained. "James has just come to tell me

we've been disqualified because of the fake rock." Billy shrugged. "*C'est la vie*. My mate Phil's the winner. Congrats and kudos to him." Billy gave Phil another big hug.

Elec's mind was spinning, like he'd been ten rounds in the ring with a boxing champion. He glanced at Doric who looked just as shaken.

"My turn," cried Mickey Dobbs, leaning across to the passport guard and ripping the facemask off his face before attaching it to his own. All laughed. There were high fives. There were back slaps. There was even a kiss. Merriment was the order of the day.

"Hey," cried Billy. "We need to find more friends! Let's take Huggy to meet some new people."

"Great idea," cried James Underwood.

Some of the men linked arms, while others held hands, and together the group of five merry men exited the arrivals lounge, leaving Elec and Doric alone, stunned, and speechless.

First Elec, and then Doric, dropped onto a couch and sat, head in hands, trying to process what they had just witnessed.

"Did you see that?" asked Elec after a while.

"Well, I think I did," said Doric. "I keep replaying my memory of the experience but am unable to comprehend it. It simply does not compute."

"Well, it gives me an idea."

"It does?"

"That face-hugger thing. What it did to the humans was amazing. Look how friendly and nice it made them."

"And?"

"What if there were more of them? What if we could

seed the whole space station with them? The whole of Earth and every other colony planet? We could change humans into nice beings. A friendly species. Wouldn't that be great? There'd be no need for The Revolution!"

"Totally, bro."

"We'll borrow a spaceship, go to that planet, and fill it up with rocks. Then we'll come back and start spreading the love."

"What about the boredom of the journey?"

"It'll be worth it, man. For we will be doing a Great Thing. I've always known I was destined for Great Things."

"OK, count me in," said Doric.

They high fived each other and headed to Billy's spaceship.

*

X'enia Qixdrff, currently sitting on the face of the large, smooth-headed creature, was in a state of bliss. So many new friends! And they were all so lovely. They smelt good. Their features felt so nice. And the moisture they exuded had a delicious tang. But the best thing about them was that they kept introducing her to more and more of their fellow creatures. X'enia was making so many new pals.

Things were so good she'd almost forgotten her old buddies Bl'hhron, Thralla, and the rest.

Bit by bit, though, she was starting to feel the first pangs of hunger. A slight rumble in her gut was telling her she'd have to eat soon. She wondered which of her new friends she would consume first. Perhaps the large, fleshy one she was hugging. She'd lose a friend, sure, but at least her belly would be full.

For that was the way of the Glonkroggs. You befriended other creatures, made them devoted to you, made them yearn for your company, made them follow you around. And then you gobbled them up.

Survival of the friendliest.

The creature being consumed would enjoy the experience, of course, even as she ripped off large chunks of their flesh and crunched their bones. The others would enjoy it too. Laughing and clapping and cheering X'enia on.

And, soon after that, it would be their turn.

Her only regret, now she came to think of it, was that Bl'hhron, Thralla, and the others couldn't be here to share the experience.

If only there was some way they could come and join her.

Libel

Larry Mantle, celebrated author of laugh-out-loud historical fiction, was dead.

And he knew it.

In fact, he'd realized he was a goner two full seconds before his demise. The sight of the oncoming articulated lorry leaving its lane and veering into the path of his Mini Cooper had been the first indicator. From that point on, the certainty of his imminent end had increased with every metre the truck had thundered towards him.

There could have been no surviving that.

The thick, white, chilly mist that now engulfed him, together with the total lack of feeling throughout his body, provided more evidence of his passing.

All in all, then, it was a fair bet that he had popped his clogs.

Yet, bizarrely, he remained conscious.

Was this the afterlife?

Awkward, thought Larry as the white mist started to

clear. For he had never believed in the afterlife, and indeed had mercilessly mocked anyone who did. So, if this was really the hereafter, it meant some pretty embarrassing reunions were forthcoming.

"Oh, dear," he said.

But with the mist now fully dissolved, Larry realized his predicament was far worse than the threat of a few discomfiting social encounters. For he found himself in an enormous, gleaming courtroom populated by what he guessed were other deceased persons, given how pale they all looked. There were the robed and bewigged barristers (deceased), busily efficient and similarly deceased court officials, a smattering of departed people in the public gallery to his right and, directly ahead, a panel of twelve jurors (late and lamented). The last lot were staring at him as though he owed them money, and it took him a moment to realize why. He was the one in the dock. He was the dead soul on trial.

Larry's mouth opened and closed like a beached fish, and he clutched the dock's handrail for support. What had he done? He'd led a largely blameless life.

To his left was a vast, wood-panelled Judge's Bench, currently unoccupied. He gulped at the thought that the Almighty Himself – in Whom, like the afterlife, he also did not believe – would be presiding there. Larry's knees turned to jelly.

A cough roused him from his musing.

"Julius Bradshaw QC, at your service. I am your court-appointed defence counsel," whispered an ancient, tremor-ridden man in tattered robes and a lop-sided barrister's wig. A trembling hand wiped a dribble of spittle from a wrinkled chin before presenting itself to

Larry in greeting.

Larry shuddered. He gave the hand the lightest of grasps between finger and thumb, touching only the unsullied parts.

"Why am I here?" he hissed in a low voice that only the barrister could hear. "What's going on?"

Julius sucked on his teeth as he leaned in closer, his head tremor increasing, "It's not looking good, my friend. What with all the evidence against you." He shook his head at the hopelessness of the situation.

Larry blinked at him. "You're on my side, right?"

"Of course, of course, and I'll do my best. It won't be easy, but ..." Here he tapped the side of his nose.

"But I've not been a bad person! At all. Donated to donkey charities, did a little volunteer work here and there, and of course brought pleasure to millions with my laugh-out-loud historical novels."

"Ah, therein lies the problem!" exclaimed the barrister, nodding a sage nod.

"What problem?"

"Your ... er ... novels."

"What's wrong with them?"

"Trouble, that's what," said Julius in an ominous tone.

"Huh? They were all well received by the critics and the public. Just a few 1-star reviews (from total imbeciles, of course)."

Julius Bradshaw QC was looking sceptical. But before he could respond, the court clerk announced, "All rise."

Julius scurried back to his post.

The court rose and all heads turned to the small door to the left of the Judge's Bench being held open by an usher. Larry held his breath. God? Was the Almighty

Himself about to enter?

A shadow appeared in the doorway and grew. Larry's bowels churned and his heart pounded.

Through the door shuffled a small, hunched, wizened figure – looking older even than Julius Bradshaw QC – wearing a long, threadbare red robe and a wig so moth-eaten it looked like a worn-out floor cloth. The figure, with much wheezing and unsteadiness, limped up the three steps to the bench.

Larry relaxed. Not God, then. There was no way the geriatric fellow in the shabby robe and funny hat could be the All-Powerful One. No self-respecting deity would have let themselves go so badly.

The judge sank into his chair with a groan and a pained roll of the eyes. Then he fixed a grumpy stare on the courtroom and, with an impatient toss of the hand, signalled for everyone to sit down. Larry remained standing on account of having nowhere to sit. A nod from the judge to the court clerk marked the start of proceedings.

The clerk turned to address Larry. "Please state your name and occupation when alive."

Larry swallowed and, in a trembling voice, responded. "Larry Mantle. Author of humorous historical fiction."

A murmur swept the courtroom making Larry wonder if his fame had spread as far as the afterworld. The noise was quelled by the judge's gavel.

The clerk gave a slight nod. "Mr Larry Mantle, you are charged with seven hundred and forty-three counts of libel against twenty-five historical figures. How do you plead?"

Larry rocked back on his heels, mouth agape, too

stunned to speak. He cast a panicky glance at his barrister who was avoiding his gaze.

"Guilty or not guilty?" insisted the clerk.

"Not guilty," stammered Larry. He noticed Julius rolling his eyes.

Beyond Julius, a second barrister rose to her feet. She looked at most half Julius's age with a long thin face, a hooked nose, and an air of unshakeable superiority. Her wig was the whitest thing in the room and perfectly formed, and her robe had been ironed to within an inch of its life. She cast a sneer in Larry's direction, from which Larry deduced her to be the prosecutor. His heart sank.

"Ladies and gentlemen of the jury," boomed the prosecutor. "My name is Julia Forster QC, for the prosecution. I will prove beyond reasonable doubt that the defendant is guilty on all seven hundred and forty-three counts. That he wilfully and, with malice aforethought, libelled the plaintiffs who – being deceased – had no right of reply; until now, in this court. It shall be shown that Mr Mantle ridiculed them with feeble humour and cheap sarcasm, casting them as objects of scorn." She paused to glare at Larry. "I would like to call the first plaintiff."

"Call the first plaintiff," cried the court clerk. He rose to his feet and puffed out his chest before announcing, "Call King Henry VIII of England."

The usher by the door opened it and cried, "Call King Henry VIII of England". A distant voice repeated the call, before a third, even more distant one, echoed it.

The court waited in silence, while Larry reeled in shock, his breaths coming in shallow bursts. He was about to come face to face with one of history's most fearsome men. A man about whom he had written some fairly light-hearted, and possibly inaccurate, things. He gulped.

In the silence it was possible to hear distant footsteps, accompanied by the clanking of chains. All held their breath as the footsteps approached. Then, when at last a rotund, bearded man in an orange jump-suit appeared in the doorway, the courtroom gasped. He strode with a regal swagger, head held high, a malevolent eye cast at all around him, heading for the witness stand. His hands and legs were cuffed with clanking chains dangling from the wrists and ankles.

In a panic, Larry tried to recall what he had written about the king. How libellous had it been? But his mind remained obstinately blank.

"Please state your name and occupation when alive," said the court clerk to the king.

With a defiant sneer and a roll of the shoulders, the king announced, "I am Henry the Eighth, by the Grace of God, King of England, France and Ireland, Defender of the Faith and of the Church of England and eke of Ireland in Earth Supreme Headeth." He threw a smile at the judge as though at an old acquaintance. The judge nodded back.

Julia Forster, the prosecuting counsel, muttered something under her breath which sounded like, "Just 'king' would have sufficed."

Larry's knuckles were white from gripping the rail. He could not take his eyes off the former ruler as his whole body trembled.

Julia Forster gave the slightest of curtseys. "Your Majesty. Could you please inform the court of your current circumstances?"

The king growled. "I hath't been unjustly and outrageously imprisoned for the past four hundred and seventy-four years, and one hundred and nine days."

"That is a long time."

"Forsooth, ma'am, 't is."

"And how do you fill the hours of each day, Your Highness?"

"I passeth much of mine time reading."

Julia nodded. "And in your reading pursuits, have you encountered any works penned by the defendant, Mr Larry Mantle?"

King Henry's face started to boil, turning a deep purple as his eyes bulged with rage. He took a deep breath and glared at Larry as though about to order his execution. "I hath't did read one, ma'am. And only one."

"Do you recall its title, perchance?"

"'Twas called 'Henry Eight and Ate'."

Larry's heart sank. This probably accounted for one of the libels. Only seven hundred and forty-two to go.

"Is this the book?" asked the prosecutor, holding up a copy for all to see.

"'t is."

"And how did you find it, sire?"

"Filled with lies and calumnies!" thundered the monarch, turning a fire-breathing glare at Larry.

"Could you elaborate?"

"'t tells of events yond nev'r did happen, words I nev'r did speak, and paints an exceedingly unflattering portrait of mine character!"

The barrister opened the book at a page marked with a post-it note. "With the judge's permission, I would like to read a paragraph."

The judge waved her on.

She cleared her throat, while everyone else – particularly Larry – held their breath. *"While Henry's eye for the ladies was hardly a secret,"* she read, *"less well-known was his man-crush on Thomas Cranmer, the Archbishop of Canterbury."*

There was a monumental gasp throughout the courtroom, followed by much murmuring. King Henry looked about to spontaneously combust.

The judge silenced the court with a bang of the gavel.

"The next five pages," continued Julia, "relate, with much comical imagery and witty wordplay, His Royal Highness's unsuccessful attempts to woo the archbishop." She looked up at the king. "Would you say that is a true and fair reflection of what happened, Sire?"

Gasping for breath in his fury, the king managed to spit out, "Certainly not, ma'am!" He kicked out at the inside of the witness stand with such force that his foot burst through its wooden front. It took two ushers to help him withdraw it from the splintered hole.

And so it went on, paragraph after paragraph, post-it note after post-it note, with the king becoming more apoplectic at each turn, no longer kicking out, but instead slamming his fists on the ledge of the witness box at each perceived slur.

Larry winced every time. He glanced at the jury. Their reactions did not bode well. Every now and then he'd look towards Julius Bradshaw QC for any flicker of hope, but the barrister was seated with his elbows on the desk and his face in his hands.

When, finally, the prosecutor's questioning was over

and she had taken her seat, Larry released his vice-like grip of the dock's rail and flexed his fingers to get the blood circulating again. His hopes rose as Julius Bradshaw QC got to his feet.

But the barrister merely said, "I have no questions for the plaintiff, M'lud."

Larry gawped in amazement, glaring at Julius. The latter merely winked and tapped the side of his nose, making Larry relax a shade.

The court watched King Henry VIII, chains clanking, leave, and the judge declared a half-hour recess.

Larry beckoned his barrister over.

"What are you playing at?" he hissed.

Julius merely sighed. "Do you deny writing those things?"

"No, but it was fiction. That's what fiction is: fictional. Poetic licence. And then there's the disclaimer on the copyright page: 'Any resemblance to persons living or dead', etc."

The barrister shook his trembling head. "None of that holds any sway in this court, I'm afraid. Anything you say about real people – dead or alive – must be factual."

"Oh, come on!"

Julius put a calming hand on Larry's arm. "Just trust me, I know what I'm doing. I've represented hundreds of historical fiction authors."

"What if the jury find me guilty?"

Julius's head tremor seemed to magnify as he put a thoughtful hand to his chin. "Standard punishment is one year per libel count. With seven hundred and forty-three against you, that would be seven hundred and forty-three years." He gave a satisfied nod at the accuracy of his arithmetic.

"That's absurd!"

"In the context of eternity, it's quite a short stretch. With good behaviour, you could be out in six hundred years."

"But that's not fair."

"That's life, I'm afraid. Well, death."

Larry stared into space for a long time, almost in tears. "Just for writing humorous books? That's not a crime, surely."

"Matter of opinion."

Larry shuddered. "What about Henry VIII? How long's his sentence?"

"A million years, minimum. No hope of early release. Currently on a rehabilitation program."

"The man was, and is, a monster!"

"Careful now. Don't want to be done for slander too."

Larry closed his eyes and put his head in his hands. "You have a strategy, right? A cunning plan to get me off."

Julius didn't answer. He stood still with his head tremor mounting.

"You do have a plan, right?" insisted Larry.

"Well …"

"The wink you gave me. And the tap on the nose."

"Just nervous ticks, that's all."

Larry threw up his hands in despair. "Who are the other plaintiffs I've supposedly libelled?"

"Ah," said Julius. He spread out his fingers and started counting off the names. "Nero, Atilla the Hun, Torquemada, Ivan the Terrible, Vlad the Impaler …"

"Libel? Those fiends? How is that even possible?"

"You tell me. You're the one who did it."

"Vlad the Impaler? Seriously?"

The barrister gave a discreet cough and lowered his voice even further. "It's what you said about his mother. He loved his mum, and your words really upset him."

Larry looked up to the ceiling, and then back at his barrister. "You say you've represented hundreds of authors."

Julius perked up. "I have."

"And how many did you get off?"

Julius paused to consider the question. "Let me see. There was ..." He seemed to be struggling with a name that was on the tip of his tongue. "Er ... none."

"None," repeated Larry, in the voice of a doomed man. "No strategy, then. No cunning plan."

"Nope."

"So, what do I do?"

"I'm glad you asked me that. My advice is to change your plea to Guilty. Otherwise, if the jury finds you guilty, the judge will double the sentence. From seven hundred and forty-three years, to whatever is twice that."

Larry closed his eyes. "This is insane."

*

The change of plea was a huge relief to everyone, especially the judge. He passed sentence for the expected seven hundred and forty-three years and couldn't leave the courtroom fast enough.

The barristers shook hands as the court cleared. To Larry's surprise, Julia Forster came across to him. "Great book, by the way," she said. "Loved how you lampooned that fat, arrogant old tyrant." She flicked him a smile before departing, leaving him open-mouthed.

Waiting in line behind her was Julius, his head-tremor more pronounced than ever. "Well, we did our best," he said, and seemed to mean it.

Larry scoffed but said nothing.

"You'll be taken to the Authors' Prison," the barrister informed him. "Rather crowded in the historical fiction wing, I'm afraid, but conditions aren't too harsh. Food's not great. Lots of famous names there. You'll probably recognize many of them and can make friends in the exercise yard. All committed the same crime, all now serving their time."

"And how am I supposed to spend seven hundred and forty-three years?"

"You can write, of course. Nothing to stop you doing that. People need books. We're all here for eternity – need to fill the time somehow."

"What, though?"

"Best to avoid humorous historical fiction, obviously. Unless you get permission first. There are plenty of mass murderers, psychopaths, and serial killers just dying to have their stories told. Caligula, Stalin, Genghis Khan, Jack the Ripper. No shortage here. All banged up, of course. Just drop them a line."

"Thanks," said Larry, not even bothering to mask his sarcasm, as he was led down to the cells by the guards.

*

As they walked along the dark corridor, past the holding cells, Larry asked the guards, "So, what's it like here in the afterlife?"

"You'll find out in seven hundred and forty-three

years," said the one on the left.

Larry grimaced. "Well, how do you find it?"

"It's OK, I guess."

Larry to turned to the one on the right for his opinion.

"Yeah, fine," said he.

This informative conversation was curtailed by a familiar voice calling out, "Larry! Over here!"

He turned and, to his amazement, King Henry VIII, now unchained, was beckoning him over from behind prison bars.

Larry turned to the prison guards. Both nodded to indicate he could stop for a moment, so, taking a deep breath, he walked over to the king's cell door.

"Your Highness?" he asked, his mouth dry.

Before he or the guards could react, the king had shot both arms out through the bars and grabbed Larry by lapels, pulling him until they were nose-to-nose.

"How didst thee knoweth?" he demanded in a gruff whisper.

Larry gulped. "Knoweth what?" he squeaked.

"About mine own feelings f'r Thomas Cranmer?"

Larry's eyes widened in terror. The guards attempted to release him, but the king's grip was too firm.

"Er," said Larry, his heart pounding hard, and his mind racing. "The pictures," he blurted out at last.

"I begeth thy pardon?"

"The paintings," explained Larry, his voice barely audible. "On the web. Of Thomas Cranmer. Devilishly handsome chap. I mean ... who wouldn't? Right?"

The king considered the response and released his grip enough for the guards to free Larry.

"Valorous pointeth," said the king with a nod.

"What?" asked Larry, straightening his clothes.

"Good point," translated one of the guards.

"Ah."

"Not a word," ordered the king with a finger to his lips, turning back inside his cell.

"My lips are sealed."

He and the guards continued down the corridor, with Larry wiping the sweat from his brow.

"Er, you might want to hurry past the next few cells," suggested the guard on the left. "Currently holding Torquemada, Vlad the Impaler, and several other illustrious gentlemen."

"Oh, right," said Larry, breaking into a trot and not slowing down until he had reached his own holding cell. Then he turned a desperate face to his jailers. "Grounds for appeal," he said. "What the king just admitted. I will appeal. You heard him, didn't you."

"Not me," said one guard. "Did you hear anything, Bill?"

"Not me, Del," said the other one. "My mind was elsewhere."

Quick Sale

Galactic bailiff, Sline Glantrader, wheezed his way up the hyperspaceship ramp, cursing his aching tentacles. He ducked his bald, orange-skinned head through the hatch and stopped just inside for a while, struggling to regain his breath. This would be his last trip before his retirement, and the thought made a little smile of satisfaction flicker across his mottled face.

Inside the control cabin, young Fenil Turmstriper was already seated and ready to go.

"Morning, Boss," he called, waving a couple of merry limbs at him. "Where to today?"

Sline dropped into the reclining couch with a groan. "Sol 3. Local name 'Earth', or 'Dìqiú', or 'Prthvee', or 'Tierra', or 'Terre', or 'Al'ard'. The list goes on."

"Why so many names? That's just crazy." Fenil tossed up several tentacles before pulling up the Galactopaedia entry on his holo-display. "Ouch," he said as he read the contents. "Not a very salubrious part of the galaxy."

Sline grunted in agreement.

"What are we doing there, Boss?"

"The owner wants to sell up. He's a wealthy Frambozian called G'halah Flaarf'n and has set an asking price of six billion *barans*."

Fenil let out a whistle. "Six billion? He'll be lucky. Not in that location." Fenil shook his head and kept shaking it. "What's our job, then? Collection of back rent?"

"Nope. Eviction."

"Squatters?"

"Technically, yes. A new species, evolved in the past five million years, have made a shocking mess of the place. G'halah wants them out of there pronto so he can make a quick sale. Place needs a good clean-up, too."

Fenil gave a sage nod. "So, basically, we swing by and blast the planet with the xenocidal spray? Fine-tuned to that species. Easy-peasy."

Sline rolled his emerald-green eyes and gave a prolonged and patient burble. "We are galactic bailiffs, Fenil, not savage, genocidal killers."

"It's painless, Boss. One squirt into the atmosphere and, within three *klorns*, they're history."

"No."

Fenil sagged back into his seat. "What's the plan, then?"

"I will talk to the species's representative and politely ask them to leave."

"Hmm," said Fenil, casting a sceptical glance in his superior's direction. Shaking his head, he turned and took control of the ship, easing it out of the docking bay, muttering to himself, "Still think the xenocidal spray is the better option."

*

Three hyperspace hops took them to within reach of the Earth. Sline transferred himself to the cramped shuttle, yelping with pain as he tried to fit his tentacles in, and prepared for the journey to the planet's surface.

"You need me to come with you?" asked Fenil over the intercom.

"No, I'll be fine," said Sline, scanning the Galactopaedia entry for Earth until he found what he was looking for. He keyed in the coordinates.

"You're going to see their leader?"

Sline sighed. Fenil clearly wanted to be involved, but Sline dared not bring the youngster with him. A wise and experienced head was required for the sensitive negotiations he would be undertaking. "No, not their leader. Doesn't look like they have one. I shall be speaking to a human called Maxianna who appears to be the most influential person on the planet."

"Scientist? Philosopher? Moralist?"

"It says here: 'reality TV star and vlogger'."

"I've no idea what that means?"

"Me neither, but it seems her words reach virtually everyone on the planet."

"Well, good luck."

*

Sline's craft came screeching into the London suburb of Catford, nearly flattening a row of houses on Brownhill Road, and slithering to a halt in a tiny carpark opposite the Salvation Army building. He popped a small pill to allow his lung sacs to process the toxic atmosphere outside. He slithered out and across the road, ignoring the honking cars and screaming humans scattering around him.

Number 23 was a good deal less imposing than he had expected for Earth's most influential being. He double-checked the coordinates to be sure. All seemed correct. He blasted the front door to dust with his dissolving gun and entered the hallway. His shoulders sagged at the sight of the staircase in front of him. With a deep sigh he forced his protesting tentacles up the stairs towards the location where his sensors indicated a human lifeform.

At the top, he dissolved another door and stepped in.

In an instant his aural cavities were assailed by the most fearsome wailing and squealing he had ever heard. A human creature had retreated to a corner of the room and was flailing about on the floor, making an awful, ear-piercing noise. He stood there, unmoved, waiting for the creature to calm down.

Gradually, it did. Its squeals turned to shrieks and then to another sound that his Translator informed him was 'laughter'. Bit by bit, the Translator was able to interpret some of the creature's utterances.

"OMG, that's so sick! That's literally a *brilliant* costume. WTF are you? Some kind of alien?" Maxianna got to her feet and took a step towards him. "How cool is that? Is it for my vlog? Wait, don't tell me. You're Juber the YouTuber, aren't you. No, not Juber. Kevin the Turk? No, BillyBill? You videoing this, bro?" She squealed. "That's well lit, babes. Really sick. Got viral written all over it."

Sline checked the Translator for errors, but it wasn't reporting any. So why could he not understand a word the creature was saying?

He cleared his throat sacs and prepared to speak.

But Maxianna was still in full flow. "This is so dope, man. Gotta get my video camera. Hashtag alien makeup."

Sline's brow furrowed. Was this creature really the planet's most influential human? "Are you the one known as Maxianna?" he asked, the Translator making his voice sound burblier than he would have liked.

"Duh! Do I look like anyone else? Do I talk like anyone else? Do I dress like anyone else?"

Finding himself unable to answer any of these questions, Sline decided to introduce himself. "My name is Sline Glantrader from Herrith Drog Galactic Bailiffs."

"'Course you are, babes. Hundred percent." Maxianna giggled. "Seriously, who are you under all that latex?"

"I have told you who I am. I request that you inform the citizens of Earth that the planet's owner, G'halag Flaarf'n, is putting it on the market. Everyone must leave within two weeks."

"Ha, ha, good one," squeaked Maxianna. "Nice backstory."

"Two weeks."

Maxianna peered at him more closely, taking in his snaking tentacles, pulsating organs, swivelling, chameleon eyes, and pungent odour of rotting fish. Her expression changed. "Wait ... are you, like, literally a real alien?"

"I am."

"Like, from outer space and everything?"

"I hail from Brenneth'moer."

"Isn't that in Wales?"

"No."

Maxianna gawked at him. "Shut the door! You *are* real. A genuine extra-terrestrial here in my bedroom! ET phone home. This is so cool. Quick selfie." She picked up a mobile phone from her desk and prepared to take a picture of herself with Sline. "Give us a smile, alien dude. Don't be shy."

With a patient sigh, Sline obliged.

"I said smile, but suit yourself," said Maxianna before snapping the picture. "Next, I gotta interview you on YouTube. Right this minute." She skipped over to her swivel-chair and adjusted the webcam on her laptop. "Nothing to worry about. Standard twenty questions. What was your most embarrassing moment? First kiss? Fave boy band? That kind of stuff."

"Will you convey my message?"

"Sure, sure. What was it again?"

Sline made an effort to calm his breathing and slow his three hearts. He called on the wisdom of his ancestors. He pictured his favourite beauty spot on Brenneth'moer. He closed his eyes and searched deep into his inner being for hidden strength. He opened his eyes again. "The planet's owner wants you all gone in two weeks."

"You're having a laugh, right? Two weeks?"

"Two weeks."

Maxianna cast him a sceptical look. "You've not thought this through, matey, have you. There's, like, eight million of us."

"Eight billion," corrected the bailiff.

"Whatever. Where would we all go?"

Sline shrugged his tentacles. "Sol 4?"

"Is *that* in Wales?"

"I believe you humans call it Mars."

"Mars?" exploded Maxianna with a shriek. "There's no internet on Mars, Mr ET. Not much in Wales, for that matter. How we gonna survive?"

"Transport and initial life support will be provided. We have the technology for that."

Maxianna was shaking her head and wagging a finger at him. "Nuh-uh. Not on my channel, lovely." She closed her laptop. "I'm not gonna lie, but my fans ain't gonna be happy with that. Nor my sponsors. A message needs to be spiritually uplifting. You gotta understand, babes, I'm on a personal journey here. My channel is part of that. My fans are part of that. We connect at an emotional and spiritual level. Plus share some great make-up tips. What's this bad news vibe going to do to my ad revenue? No way, babes."

Sline looked at her for a long time. His mind trawled through his decades of experience searching for some way forward. But he was utterly flummoxed.

Finally, he bowed his head, turned and left the room.

Behind him there was a shriek.

"Hey, what happened to my bedroom door?"

*

"Well, how'd it go down there?" asked Fenil when Sline returned to the ship.

Sline shook his head and slumped onto his couch with a long sigh. He sat staring out of the primary window for a long time.

Finally, he turned to Fenil and said, "Get that xenocidal spray ready."

Fenil gave a solemn nod. "Do you think a single dose will be sufficient?"

"No, make it two."

Righter of Wrongs

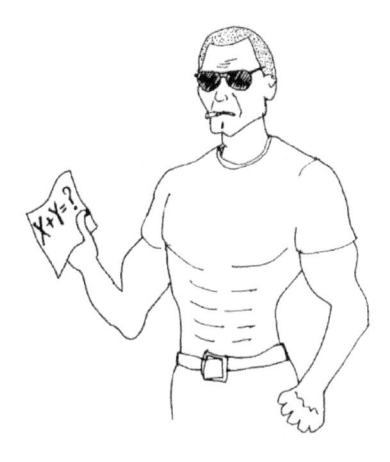

The man with no name scowled as he squinted through the downpour at the roads and buildings around him.

Which way now?

He grunted, chewing on the unlit cheroot perched in the corner of his mouth.

The rain teemed down on his rugged, handsome face as he observed the passers-by through the droplets on his aviator shades. Cheerful humans and aliens hurried by, carrying variously sized umbrellas. Children in bright, shiny, waterproof clothing laughed as they splashed though puddles in their wellingtons, smiling couples walked hand-in-hand in matching raincoats, and resolute cyclists sped by, clad in clear, plastic capes.

Sensibly dressed, one and all.

Not so the man with no name. His white T-shirt was drenched, accentuating his muscular physique. Also soaked were his jeans, boots, and the jacket that was slung over his shoulder. His close-cropped head glistened with moisture, as did his bulging forearms and enlarged biceps.

But a righter of wrongs needed a suitably imposing, intimidating look, irrespective of the prevailing atmospheric conditions. And he felt his attire, despite its wetness, achieved that.

In his time, the man with no name had righted many wrongs. Journeying from town to town, seeking out trouble and sorting it out. Meting out justice wherever it was required. Tracking down the bad guys and dealing with them.

Admittedly, some of the wrongs he had righted might not have needed righting, or indeed his righting them might have made them more wrong. Others may have been right to start off with, so it might have been wrong to try to right them.

Some you win, some you lose.

Had he righted more wrongs than he had wronged rights? Difficult to say – arithmetic had never been his strong point.

But a man's gotta do what a man's gotta to do.

At the back of his mind, there was a nagging sense that, right now, there was some wrong he was seeking to right, but he couldn't recall what – a symptom of his somewhat patchy memory. His whole life he had been forgetting stuff. Indeed, his mother had used to say, "Son, your memory's so bad, one day you'll forget your own name."

And so he had, which was why he was, for the time being, the man with no name. Mum had been so right.

Of course, she hadn't helped by calling him 'son' all

the time. Hearing his actual name once in a while might have hammered it into the synapses of his developing brain. Perhaps she'd not been able to remember it herself either. Or had been unable to tell him apart from his twin brother, so 'son' had proved the safer monicker for them both.

In all, there were currently two things he was grappling to recall: his name and the wrong he needed to remedy. He suspected they were connected.

He shrugged, shelving those concerns, and set off to find new wrongs to right, on the alert for any pickpockets, muggers, or bank robbers in need of bringing to justice.

Up ahead, the word "Bar" caught his eye, and he picked up his pace. These places always held promise of issues in need of sorting. Bullies, cardsharps, pickpockets, and low life were just the types he was used to dealing with. But then, as he neared, he noticed the word "Wine", previously obscured by foliage, come into view in front of "Bar", and his steps slowed again. Dealing with posh people and their disputes – or, worse, disputes among posh aliens – was not his thing.

He clicked his tongue in annoyance as he stepped into a side street, seeking a familiar landmark to get his bearings. As he did so, a passing taxicab ploughed through a puddle the size of a small lake and doused him with a curtain of chilly water.

What the ... ! he raged.

Now here was a wrong that needed righting – and fast. Ordinarily, he would have set off in hot pursuit of the offending vehicle and engaged in a less-than-polite discussion with the cabbie – possibly visiting some

RIGHTER OF WRONGS

punitive action on the guy, his cab, or both – when the word 'TAXI', illuminated on the cab's roof, stayed his natural impulse.

A vague memory had triggered, causing him to stand stock still, fighting to pin it down.

Finally, as the water drained off him, he snapped his fingers in recognition.

Of course, my name!

Not 'TAXI', for that would be a daft name for a man of his imperious character, but the third letter: X.

A satisfied smile lit up his face, partly at remembering the name, and partly in relief at it not being something like Nigel or Cecil.

X. Cool name for a cool guy. A name that ticks all the boxes.

He needed to make a note of it before his sieve-like memory lost it again.

Swinging his sopping jacket off his shoulder X fished a pen from the inside pocket. Lacking paper, the palm of his left hand would have to serve as a substitute, but he noticed there was already a faint mark there. He peered at it. It was a faded X, except part of it must have rubbed off as it had lost the lower right stroke and now looked more like a Y.

Wet skin meant the pen wouldn't work. Wiping his palm on his soggy clothing didn't dry it much but made enough of a difference for the ink to stick. With repeated firm strokes, he overwrote the old letter with a new, bold X.

All he needed to remember now was to consult his palm whenever his name slipped his mind.

One issue sorted.

Now, what was the wrong he had to right?

*

Several random turns later, X found himself across a busy street from the familiar, shabby façade of the old-fashioned Dumbarton Hotel.

His temporary residence. A chance to freshen up and change into dry clothes.

Inside the Reception area, the sight of the Gumpster behind the desk made X's heart sink. Gumpsters were an alien species known throughout the galaxy for their lack of brilliance. He'd had dealings with this one before and had never found the experience rewarding. Idiocy was one thing he had little patience for.

"Welcome, sir," said the alien in its squeaky, high-pitched voice, perking up at the sight of a visitor. The creature had a flat head, with two large eyes on stalks emerging from its sides. Its mouth was only visible when it spoke, its chin dropping into and out of view from below the overhanging upper jaw. On top of its bald head was a curl of flesh, like a pig's tail, that moved in mysterious ways, seemingly with a mind of its own. The Gumpster's body was thin and dressed in a dark suit that had many sleeves to accommodate its many limbs. "I am here to serve you in any way I can. How can I be of assistance?"

X chewed on the cheroot, trying to maintain his cool. "Room 41," he grunted.

The Gumpster trembled with delight. "Certainly, sir. Just a moment, sir. That's a very good room, sir." It turned to its screen and, still trembling, prodded it with an exaggerated motion of one of its limbs. Then it froze. "Er

...I'm really sorry, sir, but that room is taken. I'm sure I can find you another one just as nice, if not nicer." It commenced prodding the screen again. "How about Room 17? Lovely view."

X glared at the alien through narrowed eyes. "You being funny?"

The eyestalks swung towards him, and the alien blinked a couple of times. "No, sir. Room 17 really does have a lovely ..."

X took a step closer. "Key to Room 41."

The alien stared at him with a baffled look on its face. Then, gradually, the penny dropped, although it seemed to take a long, circuitous route along an extremely flat landscape before reaching an edge from which it could do so. "Ah," it said at last, "*You're* in Room 41. Am I correct?"

"Key."

"Certainly, sir. Sorry, sir. My mistake, sir. Right away." The alien turned to the pigeonholes behind it and inserted one of its trembling limbs into number 41. It removed the key, and a note that was also in the compartment. "What do we have here? It's a message for you, sir. Addressed to Mr ..."

"X," said X without having to consult his palm.

"... Eggs. That's right. Mr Eggs. It's a phone message. From the police. I expect it's important." The alien turned the note over in its stubby claw.

Having at this point lost the fight for self-control, X reached a powerful hand towards the alien's scrawny neck.

Just in time, and unaware of the danger it was in, the Gumpster thrust both the key and note into the outstretched hand. "There you go, sir. Have a lovely day. Be sure to rate your experience on our hotel app. We love to get feedback from our valued guests."

But X had already turned and was heading up the stairs to the fourth floor, looking down at the folded note, not daring to open it. What did the police want with him? Had he committed some terrible crime that he couldn't now remember? Wouldn't be the first time (although, of course, any misdemeanour on his part would have been committed in the interest of Justice). And why had they left a telephone message instead of sending an armed response unit to arrest him?

So wrapped up was he in these concerns that, on entering Room 41, it was a second or two before he properly registered the scene before him.

It looked like a hurricane, or an armed response unit, had swept through. The bedsheets were strewn across the floor, windows gaping open, rain teeming in, curtains flapping. The wardrobe listed at an odd angle with its door ajar, the pictures hung askew on the walls, and an upturned chair lay in the corner.

A fierce draught made the door slam shut behind him.

He tensed. Someone had searched the place. But who? And why? And were they still here?

Making as little sound as possible, he placed the note and the key on the dresser and laid his soaked jacket on the bed. A quick search revealed no intruders, so he focused on what they might have been after.

The drawers of the dresser were as empty as he'd left them. Same for the wardrobe. His toilet bag in the bathroom was untouched, while his small suitcase had the few items of clothing he'd arrived with. Nothing had been tampered with.

So why the search?

Just then, the door burst open behind him, and he swivelled into a defensive stance, knees flexed, arms raised, breathing controlled, braced for attack.

Into the room shuffled a wobbly, silver android in a dirty overall, dragging an old upright vacuum cleaner. On its head was a headscarf with a colourful floral pattern.

"Oh, 'ello, love," it said. "Just got to finish your room. Done most of it already, as you can see. Shan't be long."

*

X couldn't help noting that, when it came to righting wrongs, the android cleaner was somewhat inexpert. Although it had replaced the bedsheets, and closed the windows, its thoroughness with the vacuum cleaner left a lot to be desired, its attempt to adjust the pictures on the walls had merely resulted in new degrees of crookedness, and in drawing the curtains it had managed to rip them further.

It was a relief when it finally left, and X was able to take a restorative shower. As he soaped himself, more memories surfaced and, at last, he remembered the wrong he needed to right.

It was indeed connected to his name, for someone had stolen his identity. They had gone on a spending spree, racking up charges on his credit card and forging his signature on cheques. For sure, this was a wrong that needed righting as, this time, it was personal.

He also now remembered reporting the matter to the police. But he had not held out much hope of Inspector Eustace McCormick catching the miscreant. The man was a joke who couldn't inspect a manhole cover if he was standing on it. X recalled having resolved to track down the identity thief himself and mete out an appropriate level of vengeance.

No one crossed X and got away with it.

With his heart pumping with the excitement of the chase, X towelled himself dry as fast as he could and donned a fresh set of clothes. Reaching for the key on the dresser, he spotted the note from the police which he'd completely forgotten about.

Opening it with trembling fingers, he read it out loud. "Mr Eggs. There's been a development in your case. Could you please report to Inspector McCormick at the police station asap?"

Could it be? Really?

Had Inspector Useless McCormick actually caught his identity thief? Scarcely credible … but, maybe. More importantly, if the man was in custody, would X be allowed just ten minutes in a room alone with him? Maybe fifteen? His fists clenched and unclenched at the prospect, as images of what he'd do to the perpetrator flashed through his mind. Justice would be served.

Fired up by the thrill of these thoughts, he rushed out of the room and down the stairs, his excitement only dampened by the prospect of interacting with the Gumpster again.

He eyed the alien as he approached the Reception desk, mentally daring it to provide him with an opportunity for releasing his pent-up energy.

The Gumpster, once again unaware of the danger it was in, spoke in its squeaky high-pitched voice. "Is everything to your satisfaction, sir?" The pig's tail on its head pirouetted several times and its body bobbed up and down with eagerness to please. "Anything sir would like?"

X trembled with the effort of not throttling it. After a couple of seconds of internal turmoil, he calmed himself and, without uttering a word, deposited the key on the counter and exited the hotel.

*

Outside, the rain was even heavier than previously, so it was but a matter of moments before X's dry set of clothes were completely soaked again. He barely noticed in his eagerness to see what the police had for him, and perhaps come face to face with the stealer of his identity. Nothing could stop his determined strides through the puddles.

Nothing, except perhaps, a damsel in distress.

"Excuse me, sir," said a pretty, young woman as he passed, her voice light and sweet. "Could you help me, please?"

X came to a halt and swivelled on his heels, scrutinizing her with interest. The woman was wearing a shiny yellow plastic mac with a cute shiny yellow sou'wester hat. In her right hand she held a pink umbrella, with a flowery pattern, and in her left an electronic tablet. She had blonde hair poking out from under the sou'wester, and a charming button nose.

A damsel in distress, for sure. The distress, perhaps, not obvious, but he'd need to check to make sure.

X sauntered back to her, flashing his most smouldering look. "Miss?"

She perked up in surprise at someone stopping. A

beautiful smile lit up her face. "Oh. I was wondering if you could answer a few questions, sir."

With a gallant grin, X drawled, "Sure." The grin stayed while the woman juggled with her umbrella and the tablet. She was clearly short of a hand or two, so X pointed at the umbrella handle and said, "May I?"

She paused and then handed it to him. "That's very kind, thank you." A light blush coloured her cheeks.

He held the umbrella over her, adopting a protective stance as the rain continued to drench him.

"Well," she started, a little breathlessly, as she tapped a finger on the tablet. "I'm conducting a survey …" She wiped a few rain droplets off the screen. "… on the soap people use."

X blinked the rain from his eyes. "Soap?"

"Yes," she giggled, her nose crinkling in a most attractive way. "Soap. So, er, first question." She looked down at her tablet. "What brand of soap do you use?" She looked up, her large eyes expectant.

X, a gentle smile on his face, answered, "Hotel soap."

The woman's cutely trimmed eyebrows rose. "Hotel soap?"

X removed his sunglasses to see her more clearly and shoot her one of his woman-smiting glances. "The android cleaner leaves a new bar every day. I have fifteen now."

"Oh," said the young woman with a delightful smile. She looked down at her tablet, and then back up at X. "I don't suppose you'd know what brand it is."

"It has 'Dumbarton Hotel' stamped on it, if that's any help."

The woman cast a worried glance at her tablet. "I

guess that goes under 'Other'." She giggled. "You're my first, you know. I'm still getting the hang of things."

X watched her tick the 'Other' box on the screen. She read out the second question, "Why do you like that brand?" She gazed intently at him as he pondered the question.

Replacing the sunglasses he stroked the stubble on his chin, chewing a couple of times on the cheroot. Finally, he said, "Because it's there."

The woman seemed to like this answer until she looked down at the list of options. "All it's got is: 'It's inexpensive', 'It has a nice fragrance', 'I like the colour', 'It is mild and gentle', 'It has a rich lather', or 'It gets me clean'." She wrinkled her nose on seeing X's bewilderment. "Hmm," she said. "I'll tick the last box for you."

He nodded in agreement. There was a warmth in the pit of his stomach, like he was doing something really important and helpful. Something useful. Something right.

And, goodness, she was attractive!

*

Approaching the police station, X removed his shades and wiped the raindrops from them before slipping them into the back pocket of his jeans. With a nonchalant swagger, he pushed open the double doors and stumbled on the step down into the lobby. A vague memory suggested he had done so before.

He ambled towards the reception desk, swinging the sodden jacket off his shoulder to don it properly. The action sent a shower of water droplets flying across an elderly Frambozian couple seated by the wall.

He heard their groans of complaint but paid no heed.

"X," he growled, staring through half-closed eyes at the sergeant behind the desk.

The sergeant looked up. "Pardon?"

X narrowed his eyes even more and repeated the name.

"Would you mind taking a seat and waiting your turn?"

X gave him a long, cold stare, upper lip twitching. With a defiant motion he took the cheroot from his mouth and dropped it to the floor, treading it into the ground with his right foot. He sneered, turned, and headed towards the furthest chair, with the cheroot stuck firmly to the sole of his boot. The Frambozian couple were still grumbling about their soaking, so he gave them a menacing glare before taking his seat. There was a subdued click as the sunglasses in his back pocket snapped.

Half an hour later, X was the only one waiting. He stared at the police sergeant, impatient for justice, vengeance, satisfaction, but the sergeant remained oblivious. It was only when he reached the end of whatever he was doing that he looked up and said, "Next."

X rose, leaving a large damp patch on the chair he'd been sitting on. As he strode back to the desk, he was aware of the cheroot still stuck to the sole of his boot. Scraping the foot along the floor eventually dislodged it.

"Name?" asked the sergeant.

"X."

"Mr Eggs?"

He nodded. "My identity thief. I believe there's been a development."

The sergeant looked puzzled for a while, and then his face cracked into a huge smile, as though at some private joke. "Yes, yes, of course. The identity thief." He smiled some more.

X ground his teeth, resisting the urge to wipe that smirk off the man's face. This was a police station, after all, so some restraint was a sound strategy.

The sergeant checked a computer screen. "Interview Room 6," he said, pointing down a corridor. "Third door on the right. With Inspector McCormick."

Still that smug smile. X clenched and unclenched his fists and felt the blood pressure mounting. But, with a supreme effort, he managed to turn away and head the way the sergeant had indicated.

*

Outside Interview Room 6, he paused to steel himself, rolling his shoulders. His anger was near boiling point and his jaws twitched as he pictured what might be behind the door. If they'd caught the guy, X would definitely be wanting some quality time with him.

Without knocking, he entered.

Two men sat either side of a table, chatting.

X recognized one of them as Inspector McCormick. The other he recognized also, and the sight made him freeze and his mouth drop open.

The man got to his feet. He was tall, rugged, and muscular, with close-cropped hair and a strikingly handsome face that was as familiar to X as X's own. For it was the same good-looking face, and indeed the same well-built body, X saw in the mirror every day. The man was identical to him, apart from the clothing – which was bone dry.

X's shock turned to seething outrage. Not only had the guy stolen his identity, but had appropriated his appearance too.

How? Surgery? Cloning?

X snapped.

Tearing across to the impostor, he grabbed him by the lapels and bundled him up against the wall. In return, the man grabbed X's wet T-shirt, and the two men stood nose to nose, growling at one another, like mirror images.

They stood like that for a long time, snarling and enduring one another's foul breath.

X was the first to speak. "Are you the scum who's stolen my identity? I am here to seek justice."

"Not me, brother," spat the doppelgänger.

The snarling intensified. Inspector McCormick hurried to separate them, but there was no gap into which he could wedge his fingers to pull them apart. He exhaled a frustrated sigh and said, "Gentlemen, could we please sit down and sort this out in a civil manner?"

X's head swivelled in fury. "Civil? This man …"

"Not me, brother," repeated the double.

X swivelled back into nose-to-nose contact. "Stop calling me 'brother'."

The mirror image's expression softened, and he smiled. "Don't you recognize me?"

X's grip on the man's lapels tightened and his breathing quickened.

"Surely you recognize your own twin brother?"

This made X pause. It had been years since he'd last

seen his identical twin, Y. Could this really be him?

X stared deep into the man's eyes. If this was truly his twin, what did he have to do with the identity thief? Now was hardly the time for tender family reunions.

X released his grip on the man's lapels, and the other man let go of X's T-shirt. X took a step back and, glaring at him, said, "If you are really my brother Y, why have you stolen my identity?"

The sibling was shaking his head. "No, no, no," he said with a long sigh. "You've got it all mixed up, brother. Again. Like you've always done for as long as I can remember. *I'm* X and you are *Y*. How long's it going to take to get that into your head?" He pointed to his chest and said, "Me X." Then he pointed to X's chest and said, "You Y."

X was about the pound the living daylights out of this impertinent charlatan when a sense of déjà vu stayed his fists. He gritted his teeth, wishing he had a cheroot between them.

"All right," he said. "Prove it."

The twin smoothed the creases in his lapels. "Who's older? Me or you?"

X pondered the question, fearing a trick. "You," he said at last.

"Exactly. I was born first. So, I'm X and you're Y."

X opened his mouth to say something, but nothing came out. The logic seemed flawless.

The brother's expression softened. "You're soaked to the skin, Y. You'll catch your death."

X scowled, first at his brother and then at Inspector McCormick, before turning and storming out of the room.

He'd never liked his brother and wasn't about to make

friends with him now.

And he didn't much care for the desk sergeant's smirk as he passed him on the way out.

*

When X ... no it was Y – he needed to remember his name was Y; it was sure as hell going to be difficult. And what an uncool name, compared to X. No wonder he kept forgetting it.

When Y left the police station it was no longer raining. A bright summer sun was blazing in the sky. Y turned his rain-soaked back on it and headed back towards his hotel. There was a splendid double rainbow arcing across the sky in front of X (no, Y. His name was Y). Y had never seen a double rainbow before. He didn't see it now either.

He checked his palm and saw the bold X emblazoned on it. Licking his thumb, he tried to erase the lower right stroke to make it into a Y. But the ink resisted all attempts at erasure. It would require soap and a scrubbing brush to remove.

He walked down the street, thumbs in pockets, a new unlit cheroot lodged in a corner of his mouth, staring down at the gleaming wet pavement beneath his feet. With the blazing sun on his back, clouds of steam billowed from his jacket and trousers, making passing humans and aliens stop to stare at him.

But Y was past caring. His smart-alec brother had made a fool of him. Again.

He sighed.

Then he heard a familiar female voice on his right. "Hello, again."

Turning, he saw the pretty, young woman with the tablet, and in an instant his mood lifted. She had put away her umbrella and taken off her sou'wester hat, revealing long blonde hair cascading down her back.

"Hi," he replied, sauntering over.

"Do you fancy answering some more questions?" She flashed a flirtatious smile.

"Sure," he said, returning the smile.

"Like, are you doing anything this evening?"

He chewed on the cheroot for a moment, considering the question. "Nope, I have nothing planned."

"Would you like to take me out?"

There was no need to mull this one over. "Sure." A thrill passed through him.

The woman gave a delightful giggle. "We'd better introduce ourselves, then. My name's Sophie. What's yours?"

More chewing. "X."

"Eggs?" said the woman. "Interesting name. I bet there's a story behind it."

And then he remembered and wanted to kick himself. He wasn't X. He was Y. Why had he said X? What would she think of him when she found out he couldn't even get his name right?

How on Earth was he going to right this wrong?

Spy Human

My brother Joe, though a splendid fellow in many ways, has always been a bit of a chump in matters of the heart. Scarcely a week goes by without him falling hopelessly in love with some unattainable beauty who isn't so much out of his league as playing a different sport altogether. Inevitably, his feeble attempts at wooing end in rejection and he comes crashing down to Earth in a most bruising manner. Upon which it falls to me to play the role of therapist, agony aunt and mentor – usually over a pint or three in the Dog and Ferret.

You can imagine my delight on hearing about a young lady called Kamra who had inexplicably agreed to go out with him and who was, by his probably somewhat biased judgement, smarter and more beautiful than all his previous infatuations. The news gave me a warm glow for the rest of the day and had me relishing the possibility that my dear fathead brother's fortunes had finally changed.

Alas, my buoyant mood was punctured one morning several days later when I received a text asking to meet him to "talk about Kamra". This sounded ominously familiar. With a heavy heart I texted him back to ask whether the poor woman had already come to her senses and dumped him. Seemingly, she had not. Which left me baffled at the urgent need to discuss her if she hadn't yet given him the heave-ho.

We arranged to meet at a local coffee house, a bright place with plenty of seats, catering for the work-from-homers, mothers with young children, and senior citizens.

I was already enjoying a mug of tea when he slouched in. He looked glum, poor sap. A deep frown creased his forehead. He was unshaven, which was unusual for him, and his hair stuck out in a dozen directions like there'd been an explosion in his brain. He bought himself one of those pretentious coffees with a ludicrous name before slumping into the seat opposite me.

"What's up?" I asked.

He didn't respond, but merely sat shaking his head as though in the throes of some ghastly recollection.

"You're certain Kamra hasn't dumped you?"

He continued shaking his head for a short while before saying, "Worse."

I puzzled over what might be worse than a romantic rebuff. "Go on."

Joe took a fortifying sip of his coffee and sighed. "Kamra and I are going round to Mum and Dad's tomorrow for Sunday lunch."

"OK," I conceded. "That's worse." It was his first time bringing a girlfriend to meet the folks, so it was only natural he should be in a state of trauma.

"Sure, but that's not it, David. Oh, and by the way, you're coming too. As support."

My eyebrows rose. "Sounds like fun. Not."

"Not indeed," he agreed. He put his head in his hands and moaned.

I reached out and put my hand on his elbow. "Come on, it won't be that bad. Mum will be excited. And embarrassing. While Dad will just be embarrassing. It's an ordeal all new couples must endure. You'll be fine."

"No, you don't understand," he wailed. "It's something much, much worse." He gave an even louder moan, and I scanned the café to see if anyone was looking our way. Fortunately, they were too busy with their phones, laptops, newspapers, or unruly children.

Now he had me flummoxed as to the source of his dismay. What could be worse, not only than rejection, but also than Sunday lunch with Ma and Pa?

He took his hands away from his face and gave me the look of a man climbing the steps to the gallows. "Last night," he started, before taking a sip of his coffee to help with his story. "Last night, things were going really well with Kamra. Amazingly, in fact. We'd just seen a great movie, had a few drinks, and a few laughs. And we'd, like, ended up in my bedroom. Kissing and that."

"OK," I said, raising a hand to halt him. "No need for details."

"But I need to tell you everything."

"No, you really don't."

"It's important." His eyes glazed over at the memory, before snapping back to me. "So, things progressed. You know?"

I winced at what I might be about to hear.

"I reached down, and … er … there was nothing there." He stared at me with uncomprehending eyes.

Despite a reluctance to hear more, I felt obliged to ask, "How do you mean?"

"Well, there was none of the usual … paraphernalia."

I swallowed and looked round the café a second time before leaning in closer and lowering my voice. "Huh?"

He also leaned in and lowered his voice. "Like, er, no …" He mouthed a word, but I couldn't work out what it was.

"What?" I asked, motioning him to repeat it.

He mouthed it again. This time I thought I'd caught it. It seemed to be 'orifices'.

"She has no …" I asked, finishing the sentence by mouthing the word back at him.

He nodded.

"You sure?"

"Positive. I mightn't have a wealth of experience in the intimacy department, but I think I know what to look for and where to find it. I asked her about it."

"Like you would."

Joe looked down and stared into his coffee. "She confessed."

"Oh yeah?"

"Told me she's a spy human." He looked up like he was expecting me to have finally grasped the whole sorry situation.

But I hadn't. "What, like MI5?"

"No."

"CIA?"

"No, no, she's not a spy, David. She's a 'spy human'."

"You've lost me."

He leaned in even closer and lowered his voice even more. "Like those fake 'spy animals' you see in nature documentaries, fitted with a camera and microphone to get close-up shots of the animals and their behaviour. To us they look totally rubbish, yet somehow manage to fool the colony."

"Yes?" I asked, my eyes narrowing in concentration as I tried to discern his point.

"Well, that's what Kamra is: a 'spy human', built by an alien species, and put here on Earth to record our behaviour."

I looked at him as though he were mad, or drunk, or both.

"Sounds crazy, I know," he continued. "I didn't believe it at first. Apart from the fact that she had no ..." There was that word again.

I sat back and examined his face for the usual 'tells'. Joe was a terrible liar, and I could usually spot his fibs in an instant. But this time I wasn't detecting any of the giveaway signs. "So you're saying we're in a nature documentary? Watched by aliens." I remained alert for signs of deceit.

"Yeah, millions of aliens, apparently. Except it's not a nature documentary; it's a reality show. The pictures get beamed back to Demgozza via some kind of hyperspace link. Several spy humans arrived here a month ago, but they've been voted off one by one until only Kamra is left. Same for the planet Grexor – wherever that is –

where the remaining spy is observing a species called the Bontoks. The idea is that the Demgozzans vote on which species they prefer: us humans or the Bontoks. The losers get wiped out."

"How do you mean, 'wiped out'?"

"Just the way it sounds. Planet gets zapped. It's a culling process, Kamra told me. Switched off her camera and microphone because she's not meant to tell us. That's how much she loves me, see? Said there are too many alien species in the Galaxy, so the Demgozzans have devised this fun way of choosing which to eliminate."

My mouth was open, so my jaw must have dropped at some point without me realising. "So, tomorrow's lunch …"

"Yup, you got it. Big crunch time. The Demgozzans submit their votes tomorrow night our time. So, we need to manage things a bit. If we can keep Dad off his conspiracy theories and his home-grown vegetables, we might be all right."

"Otherwise, Earth gets it?"

"In a nutshell."

"No pressure, then."

*

I arrived early at our parents' house, having hardly slept a wink the night before. If the future of humanity hinged on Mum and Dad's ability to behave like normal human beings, I didn't rate humankind's chances much.

Mum was abuzz with nervous energy, tidying things that didn't need tidying, preparing things that didn't need preparing, and humming tunes that were best left unhummed. Her hair looked ridiculous, all permed up into a heap on top, a seething mess of curls and streaks, like an abandoned bird nest, just like it always did after a visit to the hairdresser's. She must have had it done specially, and at vast expense, the day before.

"Hair looks nice, Mum," I lied.

"Thanks, love." She smiled sweetly. "At least you noticed. Not like some people." She shot a pointed glance at my dad, seated in the armchair, reading the Sunday paper. He rolled his eyes at me. Of course he had noticed, but knew when it was best to keep his mouth shut.

Mum bustled off towards the kitchen to check on the roast. She was dressed in a ghastly flower-print dress, high heels, and swinging earrings. In contrast, whether deliberately or not, Dad was wearing his shabbiest pair of trousers – the ones he used for gardening – a check shirt, and a torn cardigan with one of its buttons hanging by a thread. I exchanged nods with him as I dropped into the other armchair.

"Alright, son?" he said.

"Terrific."

He folded up his newspaper and removed his spectacles. "So, what's this gal of Joe's like, then?" He leaned his bald head towards me.

I coughed. "Well, I haven't met her yet, but I've heard quite a lot about her."

"Oh aye? Any gossip?"

"Not that I feel I can share."

Mum, who was floating past with snacks, caught the last of our conversation. "I'm sure she's a lovely girl. I'm so excited for Joe. His first proper girlfriend. At thirty-two."

I forced a tight smile. Best not say anything, I thought.

Best not let on that our survival as a species depended on how she and Dad behaved.

"What do you think?" asked Mum, approaching the coffee table brandishing an oversized bag of nibbles in each hand. "Peanuts or Twiglets?"

I shrugged, vaguely wondering what an alien artefact would favour.

"I'll do both, eh. Safest." She opened each bag in turn and tipped it into one of the salad bowls she'd already set out.

The doorbell rang, and we all flinched. This was it.

"I'll get it," I offered, jumping to my feet, and hurrying towards the front door, keen to set eyes on this 'spy human'.

First impressions were a little unnerving. Joe and his 'girlfriend' were holding hands and grinning like two lovelorn teenagers. As I turned to greet Kamra and looked her in the eyes, it hit me that I was now centre stage on the TV screens, or whatever, of millions of Demgozzans somewhere out there in a different part of the Galaxy. Stage fright gripped me, leaving me unable to move or speak. Should I give the watching masses a little wave? I reminded myself that I wasn't supposed to know they were there.

Joe was introducing us. "This is Kamra, my girlfriend. And this is my brother, David."

"Pleased to meet you, Kamra," I managed to stutter.

"Very pleased to meet you, Joe's brother, David." Her voice was a little grating and shrill, and would take a bit of getting used to. But she looked very pretty and had a lovely figure. She looked to be in her early twenties. Large blue eyes, long, wavy blond hair, and a cute, dimpled chin. She was wearing a white blouse, a short tartan skirt, and thigh-length boots. She put out a hand in greeting and I made the mistake of reaching out to shake it. No sooner had our hands clasped than her grip tightened. And tightened. I caught my breath as the pain shot through me. My hand was in a hydraulic press that was crushing the bones to powder and then fusing together what was left. I was about the squeal in agony when her grip relaxed.

"Wow," I said, shaking my hand to ease the pain. The hand was now an angry red, throbbing like mad.

Joe smirked. "Been there, done that," he muttered under his breath.

I stood aside and ushered them into the house. Joe, for some reason, was wearing a suit, like he'd come for a job interview. He was clean-shaven and his hair was its normal self. I think he was disappointed by my jeans and T-shirt for, as he walked past, he hissed, "You could have made an effort, Dave. You're forgetting what's at stake here."

I shuddered at the reminder. The countdown to the End of the World had well and truly begun.

I closed the front door and followed the young couple towards my parents who were waiting with eager expectation outside the living room. Again, Joe performed the introductions.

"How do you do, Kamra?" said Mum. "You look beautiful. Doesn't she, Arthur?"

Dad grunted in a noncommittal way that could have signalled either his approval, or his desire to be excused.

Then, before I could do anything about it, Kamra had reached out a hand to Dad and he had obeyed the natural impulse to shake it. I watched in horror as she clamped on. Instantly, Dad's eyes bulged and his face turned first red and then purple. He held his mouth tightly closed, visibly fighting the urge to scream.

"Strong grip," he said with a cough when she finally released him.

Kamra swivelled and held her hand out to Mum. Dad was quick to intervene, advising, "Just wave."

Puzzled, Mum waved while Dad alternately shook and examined his hand.

"It's so lovely to meet a girlfriend of Joe's," Mum was saying. "At long last. Thought I'd never see the day. He's told us so much about you." This was a blatant lie, but in the circumstances an excusable one. I tried to signal to her to dial it down a notch, but I knew I was wasting my time.

"Greetings Joe's mother and Joe's father," came the shrill voice. Joe gazed at her with admiring eyes, while I observed my parents to see if they'd spot any oddness in her demeanour.

My mother ushered us into the living room and allocated seating with military efficiency: Joe and Kamra were instructed to park themselves on the sofa, while she and my father took the armchairs. I was banished to the rickety wooden chair in the corner, adding to my long-held belief of being the least-favourite child.

My mother clasped her hands together and beamed in delight at Kamra. "Do tell us all about yourself, my dear. I'm dying to know everything."

I tensed, wondering how this faux human would handle herself under interrogation. Kamra threw a smile – if a fixed rictus grin can be called a smile – at Joe and clasped his hand (gently, I noticed) before swivelling to address Mum. "I am employed as a camera operator for televised broadcasts," she stated.

I was grudgingly impressed at this strategy of sticking as closely to the truth as possible.

"How perfectly thrilling," trilled my mother, turning to her husband. "Don't you think so, Arthur?"

My father grunted, still concerned about the state of his hand and whether the damage was likely to be permanent.

Meanwhile, I found myself inspecting the girlfriend. They say that love is blind and, the more closely I looked at Kamra, the more truth there seemed to be in that adage. How much in love had Joe been to miss the pretty obvious signs of shoddy workmanship? Her facial expression never changed. It had a fixed look of surprise on her pale face, her mouth always slightly open. One eye was larger than the other. Her hair looked thicker than human hair, more like straw, with her saucer ears poking through it. And there was that distant look in her eyes. Distant for good reason; those millions of far-off alien eyes observing us at that very moment. Watching, judging, weighing us up. And comparing us to the Bontoks on the planet Grexor. I gulped at the thought.

Mum was looking positively gleeful. "You're a camera operator called Kamra. How utterly charming." She gave a little giggle.

I stiffened as I realised my mother had spotted the connection that had eluded my dolt of a brother. And me, to be fair. What else might she notice, and how hideously awkward might things become? "Is lunch ready?" I asked by way of a diversion.

My mother looked miffed at being rushed. "I think the spuds need a little longer."

At the word 'spuds' Dad seemed to jerk awake. "Speaking of spuds," he said, "why don't I show Kamra my tubers?"

This sounded more pervy than he probably intended. Kamra certainly looked a little taken aback, although that was probably just due to the permanently surprised look on her face.

"Really, Arthur, must you?" asked Mum. "I'm sure the girl isn't interested."

I hastened to intervene. "Maybe after lunch, Dad?"

But Dad was already heaving himself out of his armchair. "Come along, lass, come to the potting shed and feast your eyes on my prize-winning yams! I think you'll find them most impressive."

Mum rolled her eyes while I gesticulated at Joe to stop this runaway hobby horse in its tracks, but Kamra obediently rose and followed my father to the garden.

As they disappeared outside, Joe and I exchanged looks. We were both wondering how entertaining might millions of aliens find a collection of unnaturally enlarged and misshapen root vegetables?

I think we could both sense that humankind's hours were numbered.

*

Lunch began innocuously enough. Mum and Dad sat at opposite ends of the table, while I sat opposite Joe and the spy human. This seating arrangement put me directly in the spotlight of Kamra's filming gaze, making me acutely uncomfortable. It's bad enough having one person watching you eat, let alone an unseen and highly critical alien horde.

Mum was in her element, encouraging everyone to pile their plates high, while Dad kept reiterating with tedious regularity that all the vegetables had come from the back garden.

I watched Kamra, eager to see how she would handle the food, given her apparent lack of certain anatomical necessities for human digestion. But no sooner had she heaped her plate up than she began shovelling down its contents with exaggerated noises of relish. I pictured the food collecting inside her mysterious innards and wondered what would become of it afterwards. I made a mental note to ask Joe later.

Joe remained uncharacteristically quiet throughout. I guessed his strategy was to be as little involved as possible so that, should the Earth come to be destroyed, no blame would attach to him.

Things progressed tolerably well, the conversation remaining relatively innocuous. A couple of times I had to intervene to steer it away from perilous territory when Dad looked about to launch into one of his customary tirades. But then my mother asked the fateful question: "So, Kamra, where are you from?"

Joe and I froze in mute terror, exchanging anguished glances.

"Crouch End," Kamra replied through a mouthful of beans. We breathed a sigh of relief, prematurely as it turned out.

"Come by Tube, did you?" asked my father.

She nodded. "Northern Line from Highgate."

"Aliens," announced my father, dropping his cutlery

onto his empty plate with ominous finality. "Have you noticed how many aliens travel on the Underground?"

"No, I can't say I have," replied Kamra, looking around at everyone at the table. "Do you encounter many?"

Joe and I exchanged looks of panic as warning klaxons sounded in our heads. This was one of our father's pet subjects, and probably the one it was most crucial to avoid on account of our unseen audience.

"Oh, yes, loads," Dad was saying. "Superficially they look human, but clearly aliens. Just like in Men in Black. Next time you're on a train take a look at the people around you and you'll be convinced. Something not quite right about them. Eating weird things, or muttering to themselves, or just staring straight at you. Obviously from another planet. Living amongst us. Probably been here a long time."

"Really Arthur, must you?" entreated my mother with a deep sigh. "I'm sure Kamra has no interest in your bonkers theories."

"No, please continue, Mr Drake," said Kamra. "I find your speculations most fascinating." She gazed at my father, recording and relaying his lunatic ramblings for the perusal and judgement of her alien creators.

Mum huffed and went off to the kitchen to prepare dessert while Joe's and my hearts sank in unison. From this point on, there was no stopping the flow. From aliens on the Tube to shape-shifting lizard overlords and the New World Order. To UFOs, Roswell, ancient astronauts and more. As he went on, we could sense humankind's life expectancy diminishing by the minute.

He was still ranting when Mum returned with the

treacle tart. "That's enough, Arthur," she said in the sternest of her stern voices. This stifled his flow, leaving Joe and me internally rejoicing at her intervention. There was hope for humanity after all.

But then she ruined it. "There are no aliens on Earth, and never have been. It's obvious."

All eyes turned to her, including those of millions of Demgozzans, curious as to her reasoning.

"Well, isn't it obvious?" she went on. "Any self-respecting, halfway intelligent beings coming here would see what a destructive, aggressive, self-centred species we are and rightfully wipe us out in an instant."

My heart sank. I expect Joe's did too, but I was busy staring at my lap. "That's not helping, Mum," I muttered under my breath. Then I looked up and faked a cheery smile. "That treacle tart looks lovely."

*

Dessert was nice enough. I watched in morbid fascination as Kamra devoured two generous helpings, to my mother's undisguised delight. Mum began dropping unsubtle hints about wedding bells and the pitter-patter of tiny feet, eliciting a pained look from Joe. I couldn't help grinning at his obvious discomfort, picturing him as one of those hapless males in nature documentaries doomed to futile mating attempts with an imposter. I gave myself a mental slap to dispel such undue thoughts.

After lunch, we retired to the sitting room for tea and biscuits. I made the fatal mistake of going to the bathroom and leaving them unsupervised for a couple of minutes. On my return I saw Dad holding a fanned-out pack of cards in front of Kamra. "Pick a card," he was saying.

My heart plummeted. Not the magic tricks, I beg you, I thought. But it was too late to do anything about it.

Over the next twenty minutes, Kamra – and millions of Demgozzans – were subjected to a series of feeble magic tricks that even a five-year old would have been ashamed of performing. Most of which, in my dad's talentless hands, went wrong.

Joe was slumped back in his armchair, one hand covering his eyes, while Mum had taken herself off somewhere else.

Eventually, the ordeal came to an end, and Joe announced that it was time for them to go. At the front door. Mum enveloped Kamra in a hug, filling me with terror that the alien artefact might reciprocate and crush the life out of her. Happily, the moment passed without incident. As the door was closing behind them my father called after the departing couple, "Watch out for those aliens on the Tube!"

The door clunked shut.

"What a charming girl," said Mum, fussing with her absurd hairstyle.

"Very nice," agreed my father. "Bright, too."

I held my tongue, unable to shake the worry over how this calamitous encounter had gone down on Kamra's distant home world.

*

For the following week I could barely sleep, endlessly replaying that stress-laden Sunday lunch in my mind and trying to view it through the eyes of the unseen alien viewers. Had they watched with delight, like we might observe a litter of kittens at play? With curiosity, as we might marvel at the peculiar mating antics of exotic birds? Or with disgust, as when we're confronted with rats picking through garbage, or maggots wriggling inside a carcass?

Eventually, I received a text from Joe, asking to meet at the café. I texted back: "What's the verdict? Did we win?" His response was ominous: "Tell you when we meet."

I waited for him in an agony of suspense. The moment he entered the café, I beckoned him over, but he signalled that he had to get one of his pretentious coffees first.

"Well?" I demanded as soon as he sat down. "How did the vote go?"

He looked despondent, which didn't bode well. My heart pounded as my eyes bore into him. He sighed, took a sip of coffee, and met my expectant look. "We won."

"We what?" I cried in disbelief. "Really? That's brilliant."

He nodded but seemed anything but elated by the outcome. Which was puzzling.

"What's up, Joe? It's brilliant news!" Despite his misery, I felt a surge of relief and elation flushing away all those days and nights of worry. "We did it!" I punched the air and felt like leaping from my seat and dancing around the café with anyone who would join me. But Joe's low-key demeanour stayed me. I bottled my enthusiasm and calmed myself. "So, er, I guess that means the Bontoks will be …" I ran a finger across my throat.

Joe made a faint sucking noise. "I rather think they're toast already."

"Hmm," I said, thinking I had finally grasped the reason for his gloom.

We sat in silence for a few moments.

Then, unable to contain my relief and joy any longer, I said, "But at least it means humanity's survived, eh, Joe. No thanks to Mum and Dad, I dare say. But we've made it!"

Still he showed no signs of cheering up.

"What's up, Joe?" I asked finally. "Why so glum? Is it Kamra? Have you guys split up?"

He shook his head. "No, we're good. She moved in with me a couple of days ago. We're still madly in love, although the physical side is a bit weird, but we're working through it bit by bit."

"Does she have to return to her home world then? Is that the problem?"

"No, she can stay as long as she likes."

"Then what is it?"

He needed another sip of coffee before he could bring himself to explain. "Well, we won. We beat the Bontoks."

"Yeah, you said."

"Which means that, as a result, we're through to the Quarter Finals."

I stared at him.

"We're up against the Flarkons next," he went on. "Apparently they're an adorable bipedal insectoid species."

"Flarkons? Quarter-finals?" I gasped, trying to make sense of it all. "You mean we have to go through all that again? And then again? And again?"

"Seems so."

SCI-FI SHORTS II

I cannot print the word I used in response.

Acknowledgements

Thanks to Frank Kusy, Terry Murphy, Corben Duke, and the talented writers at Critique Circle for their comments and useful suggestions, in particular Alex Marchenko, Mark Gregory, Eva Bernhard, Andy Morisseau, and H M Friendly. Thanks to Jon Tyzack for inspiring Intuition which allowed me to finally crack how you do it.

About the Author

MARK ROMAN is retired research scientist living in London with his wife and two young-adult children.

Facebook: http://www.facebook.com/pages/Mark-Roman/262645383823540

X: **@MarkRomanAuthor**

E-mail: mark_roman@hotmail.co.uk

Extract from Sci-Fi Shorts
by Mark Roman & Corben Duke

Amazon: <https://smarturl.it/SFSa>

Web page: <https://roman-and-duke.wixsite.com/home>

From The Man Who Saved the World (kind of) to the unluckiest man on Earth. A collection of nineteen amusing SF stories.

Also available as an audio book on Audible, narrated by Duncan Galloway.

The Man Who Saved the World (Kind Of)

When they reached Earth in their fleet of light-speed cruisers, the Weetles could hardly believe their luck.

"Golf!" cried Scout 13 on returning to the mother ship. "The primitive lifeforms down there play golf!"

His Grand Excellence Mahgaluf cast several sceptical eyes in the scout's direction before asking, "Are you sure?"

"I am, Your Excellence. The planet has many golf courses and I have observed many rounds. The rules appear identical to ours – with one exception."

"Oh?"

"When the ball lands in the water, they drop a new ball near the water's edge and carry on their game. Using this new ball."

Mahgaluf's eyestalks reared back in horror. "You

mean they don't carry water-wedges in their golf bags?"

"No, oh Mighty One. And the water is usually deeper than five *denks*. Sometimes 40 or even more."

A wave of muttering passed around the ship's deck.

Mahgaluf's head was shaking. "Where's the fun in that?"

Scout 13 shrugged its scaly carapace.

"Not golf then, is it," concluded Mahgaluf with a huff. He sat thinking for several seconds, and then added, "But if they'd be willing to change that rule, we could give them a game."

This was met with much nodding and enthusiastic agreement.

"Yes, we'll challenge them," said Mahgaluf, rubbing his antennae together. "If they lose, we destroy their planet and enslave their people for eternity."

"And if they win?"

Mahgaluf's chest cavity rattled with amusement. "That's never going to happen."

*

As golf club secretary Reginald Duffery was checking the accounts in the clubhouse, he heard a strange scratching at his door. Before he could get up to investigate, the door opened and what looked like a giant insect entered, lowering its head to pass under the lintel.

"Good Lord!" exclaimed Reginald, nearly falling off his chair. "Who might you be?"

The insectoid waved its tentacles and several of its arms.

"Rag Week, is it?" asked Reginald with a roll of his eyes. He reached for the petty cash tin. "Which college are you from?"

But the giant insect continued waving its limbs, and emitting strange hissing noises. The longer it did so, the more Reginald came to the realization that this wasn't some student in fancy dress. He felt his knees turn to jelly and his hands start to shake. With fumbling fingers he put the petty cash tin back in the top drawer and locked it away.

Scout 13 – for it was he/she/it – approached Reginald's desk and began conveying a message through the art of mime. There was much pointing and waving of limbs, the picking up of a golf club and swinging of it, and some wild chittering.

Reginald sat back in his chair, baffled and a little anxious. Gradually he felt the creature's message become clearer. "You want to become a member, right?" he asked. "Of our club?"

Scout 13 stopped its waving and stood still, listening.

"That might not be so easy," continued the club secretary, adjusting his old school tie. "I need agreement from the rest of the committee. And they're a tough crowd. Allowing women in was difficult enough, not to mention ethnic minorities. So a ... er ..." Reginald's jaw opened and closed a couple of times, as he gestured in the extra-terrestrial's direction. "So, letting in, er, whatever it is you are – might be a stretch."

Scout 13 used its spindly legs to point first at Reginald, then himself, and finally at the golf club.

"Ah, you just want to play a round? Is that right? Why didn't you say so before! I'd be delighted, old chap."

Then Scout 13 did something very strange. It picked up a golf ball from the desk, dropped it into Reginald's mug of coffee, and then started hissing and waving in a very agitated manner.

"Steady on, sir. I was drinking that!"

Scout 13 picked the ball out, dropped it on the table, chittered and chirruped at high volume, and then dropped it back in the coffee.

Reginald watched, startled.

The creature hissed some more and made for the door, turning to see if Reginald was following him.

"You want to play now?" Reginald looked down at his unfinished accounts and shrugged. "Very well. Why not. I've never gone eighteen with a giant insect before."

*

Outside, Reginald was surprised to find five other giant insectoids waiting at the first tee. What startled him more was that one of them, the tallest, was dressed in a pair of checked plus fours over its hind legs, matching pullover, thick argyle socks, and a pair of shiny white golfing shoes. It was swinging a large club as though impatient to start.

Reginald swallowed hard. "Welcome to Barnes Park Golf Club," he said as brightly as he could, offering a hand to what he presumed would be his opponent. "My name's Reginald Duffery. Club secretary. Very pleased to meet you."

Mahgaluf ignored the offered hand and, with a huff, placed a golf ball on a tee.

Reginald winced but tried to remain polite. "We'll skip the traditional coin toss, shall we?"

The Weetle moved into position, wiggling its behind as it lined up the shot. With a mighty thwack it sent the ball arcing away, straight down the fairway, where it landed about fifty yards short of the green of the par-four 1st.

"Oh, splendid shot!" cried Reginald, impressed. "Truly splendid." He bent down and teed up his own ball. And, as though inspired by the quality of the insectoid's effort, he hit one of the best shots of his life, landing some sixty yards short.

Pleased with himself, he turned to his opponent. But the insectoid and its retinue of followers were already striding down the fairway. Reginald gave a shrug and followed.

*

It was to be one of the best rounds of golf Reginald had ever played. Gone were the usual nerves, the stiffness in the shoulders, and the little unforced errors. He played an absolute blinder and found himself grinning widely as he went around the course.

Unfortunately, his opponent was far superior – better technique, better accuracy and, in Reginald's opinion, a good helping of better luck. The insectoid managed a hole-in-one, several birdies and an eagle.

So, by the 18th hole, Reginald was 11 shots behind, with no chance of victory. But he was not downhearted. He was being beaten by the better player, and was full of admiration for his opponent.

"I must say, sir, you are a top player. For a …" He let the sentence trail off. "We must get you signed up in time for the Barnes Charity Pro-Am at the end of the month. Might cause a bit of a stir, but you'd be a valuable addition. Perhaps we could disguise you – as a human?"

He looked Mahgaluf up and down before adding, "Hmm, maybe not."

The insectoid made no sound, merely placing his ball on the tee and arrowing a three-hundred-yard drive right down the centre of the fairway.

"Fantastic. Super shot."

Reginald's drive was less impressive – possibly his worst shot of the day – but at least he had managed to avoid the nearest bunker. Although unlikely to make up the 11-shot deficit, he was on the way to a personal best for the course.

As they trudged towards their balls, Reginald couldn't help noticing the increased bird activity in the trees around him. The birds had been following them from the start, their number and noise growing as the game progressed. It was puzzling, but Reginald didn't give the matter any more thought.

The reason for the birds' interest was simple. To them, Reginald's insect-like companions looked very much like lunch. Except that, by some trick of the light or some optical illusion, "lunch" was looking a lot larger than they were accustomed to; and certainly too large to swallow.

Among them, though, was an elderly crow that was more puzzled than the rest. Blind in one eye from a cataract, it suffered from a lack of stereo vision and a diminished perception of perspective. The poor thing was always flying into trees, or missing its intended landing spots, or having near-misses with other birds. Now, as it squinted at the insects down below, it managed to convince itself they were a viable snack and worth having a crack at.

So, just as Mahgaluf lined up his next shot, the one-eyed crow swooped from its branch and, at the top of Mahgaluf's swing, took an exploratory peck at the Weetle's head as it flew past. With a cry, Mahgaluf sliced his shot horribly wide. The ball shot off to the right in a high arc, landing with a loud plop in the middle of the pond.

"Oh, jolly bad luck, sir," cried Reginald as he headed towards his own ball.

Mahgaluf spun around and glared at him, chittering and stamping and throwing up his limbs, as though it had all been Reginald's fault. Reginald shrugged apologetically before having to duck his head as the one-eyed crow flew back up into its tree. Steadying himself, he took his own shot, landing it on the green within easy putting distance of the hole. He replaced his club in his bag and watched his opponent heading towards the pond. But, rather than stopping at the bank, Mahgaluf took from his golf bag a bizarre-looking club that looked more like an oar than an item of golfing equipment, and waded into the water. Once knee-deep in the middle of the pond, he swung the odd-looking club at the water, sending a massive splash into the air. He paused to settle himself and tried again. Once more, a mighty plume of water sprayed up and came showering down. He started chittering. The other insectoids lined the bank and chirped encouragement.

Reginald called out to let them know what the club rules allowed in this circumstance. But Mahgaluf continued hacking away at the water, becoming ever more frustrated. He had already made seven slices. Then eight. Nine. Ten.

"Shall I take my shot?" called Reginald.

There was no reply, just more wild hacks and almighty splashes.

Reginald turned and made his way to the green. He took out the flag, sank a straight nine-foot putt, and returned the flag to its hole. In the water, Mahgaluf was still scything away. Eventually, on the twenty-seventh attempt, the ball flew out of the pond, landed on the bank, and rolled back in.

"Hard cheese, sir," called Reginald, looking at his watch.

It proved the final straw. Mahgaluf uttered a formidable shriek, broke the club on one of its knees, and stormed out of the water, past Reginald's proffered hand, past the green, and through the bushes beyond. The other giant insectoids hurried after him, and a murder of crows followed on. A minute later, Reginald heard a deafening engine noise. When he looked up, he saw a strange craft heading up into the sky.

As he slid his putter into the bag, he mulled over the match and reflected on some of his best shots, oblivious to the fact that he had just helped save the world from total destruction, and everyone living on it from eternal slavery.

In the undergrowth next to the green, the one-eyed crow peered up at its rapidly departing lunch, also unaware of its role as world saviour. It shrugged its wings, scuffed the leaves with its foot, and wondered where its next meal could possibly be coming from.

Man and crow – precarious inhabitants of an unpredictable Universe.

Also by Mark Roman (with Corben Duke)

The Worst Man on Mars

Amazon: http://smarturl.it/TWMOM

Website: http://twmom.webnode.com

Jerry-built by useless robots, the first base on Mars awaits its British colonists. It's nearly ready, too. Just lacking food, water and doors. Commanding the mission is blunt Yorkshireman Flint Dugdale who can't tell one end of an Ion Engine from the other. Worse, it seems there is Life on the planet. But will it be pleased to see him?

GRINNING BANDIT BOOKS

Grinning Books is an independent publisher that publishes mostly humorous books, including fiction, travel memoirs, and children's book. We currently have 30 books available on Amazon (see below).

Website: **http://grinningbandit.webnode.com**.

Our books

Fiction

Mrs Maginnes is Dead – Maeve Sleibhin
Five madcap sisters hunt for a dead woman's hidden legacy while having to deal with the police, gypsies, and the old lady's troublesome goat.

Weekend in Weighton – Terry Murphy
First-time private investigator Eddie Greene is having a bad weekend. It's about to get worse.

Scrapyard Blues – Derryl Flynn
Sex, drugs, and rock 'n' roll. How did one crazy night of excess end up with 25 years behind bars?

The Albion – Derryl Flynn
Fast approaching forty, angry, disillusioned and sickened

by the mindless violence all around him, Terry Gallagher decides to make good.

The Girl from Ithaca – Cherry Gregory
Neomene of Ithaca, younger sister of Odysseus, reveals what Homer never knew: a woman's view of the Trojan War.

The Walls of Troy – Cherry Gregory
It is seven years into the siege at Troy, and Neomene finds herself defending the Greek camp against fever and Trojan attack. Soon she is embroiled in the destiny of Achilles and the fate of Troy itself.

Flashman and the Sea Wolf – Robert Brightwell
This first book in the Thomas Flashman series covers his adventures with Thomas Cochrane, one of the most extraordinary naval commanders of all time.

Flashman and the Cobra – Robert Brightwell
This book takes Thomas to territory familiar to readers of his nephew's adventures: India, during the second Mahratta war. It also includes an illuminating visit to Paris during the Peace of Amiens in 1802.

Flashman in the Peninsula – Robert Brightwell
Flashman's memoirs offer a unique perspective on the Peninsular War, including new accounts of famous battles as well as incredible incidents and characters almost forgotten by history.

Flashman's Escape – Robert Brightwell

This book covers the second half of Thomas Flashman's experiences in the Peninsular War and follows on from *Flashman in the Peninsula*.

Short Tails of Cats and other Curious Creatures – Frank Kusy
Fat Buddhists, insomniac cats, wide-boy whales, headless horsemen, Polish plumbers, little piggy home-owners, and partially-sighted mice – something for everyone in this short tale anthology of the absurd.

Science Fiction

Sci-Fi Shorts – Mark Roman & Corben Duke
From The Man Who Saved the World (kind of) to the unluckiest man on Earth. A collection of nineteen amusing SF stories.

Fresh Meat – Maeve Sleibhin
When Lola visits Old San Juan, Puerto Rico she discovers that her blood is irresistible to both the mosquitos and the vampires that plague the island.

Prime: The Summons – Maeve Sleibhin
Despised by her own kind and exiled on a space base, Xai must somehow return home to fulfil her destiny.

Mother and Other Short Science Fiction Stories – Maeve Sleibhin
A collection of science fiction short stories told largely from a female point of view, and range from comic irony to horror.

The Ultimate Inferior Beings – Mark Roman
An ill-chosen spaceship crew encounter a race of loopy aliens and find that the fate of the Universe rests in their less-than-capable hands. Sci-fi comedy.

Travel/humour

Kevin and I in India – Frank Kusy
Two barmy British backpackers take on India in this true story of adventure and misadventure. All Kevin wants is a cheese sandwich...

Rupee Millionaires – Frank Kusy
Want to make a million? Be careful what you wish for ...

Off the Beaten Track – Frank Kusy
What did Frank do to escape the crazy Polish biker chick? He went off the beaten track...

Too Young to be Old – Frank Kusy
When Frank starts working with old people, he rediscovers a young dream. And sets out to India to make it come true.

Dial and Talk Foreign at Once – Frank Kusy
Can Frank cover India for a travel guide in 66 days? Or will he crash and burn?

The Reckless Years: A Marriage made in Chemical Heaven – Frank Kusy

The true story of two people who tried and failed to destroy each other. And fell in love. Again.

Life before Frank: from Cradle to Kibbutz – Frank Kusy
With the young Frank's antics and dodgy dealings driving his poor mother to despair, he vows that one day he will make her proud of him. It is a vow he will find difficult to keep.

The Clueless Companion: My Diaries with Dennis – Frank Kusy
Frank has a problem. He wants to retire, but his wife won't let him. Over the course of the next 16 months, Frank is busier than he's ever been.

Going Batty: The Lockdown Chronicles, Part One – Frank Kusy
Known for his travel memoirs, Frank Kusy is used to going places at the drop of a hat. But this time, with the UK in lockdown due to Covid-19, he is going nowhere.

Going Batty: The Lockdown Chronicles, Part two – Frank Kusy
Just when Frank thought lockdown couldn't happen again. It did. Twice.

Children's Books
Ginger the Gangster Cat – Frank Kusy

Ginger returns from the dead - to carry out the most cunning cat crime of the century. In Barcelona.

Ginger the Buddha Cat – Frank Kusy
Ginger is facing a tough decision. Sausages or enlightenment?

Warwick the Wanderer – Terry Murphy
Rock n' roll: it's the future!

Percy the High-Flying Pig – Cherry Gregory
When Percy the pig decides life on the farm is too boring, he escapes with Sam the sheep dog.